Will's Changing World

Wishing you
all good things
in your world.
Susan Tuttle

Will's Changing World

...

Susan Tuttle

ISBN: 1530367735
ISBN 13: 9781530367733
Library of Congress Control Number: 2016904141
CreateSpace Independent Publishing Platform
North Charleston, South Carolina

Author's Note

• • •

WILL'S CHANGING WORLD IS A work of fiction set around actual events leading up to the bombardment of Fort Sumter in Charleston Harbor in 1861. Although most of the characters are fictional, I include several based on real people who were involved directly or indirectly with these events. These are Major Robert Anderson, who was the commander of the garrison assigned to protect and maintain the harbor; Lt. Jefferson Davis and Pvt. Daniel Hough, who were serving in the garrison; and Lt. Davis's sister, Annie Davis, who was attending a lady's finishing school in Charleston.

I have attempted to show the reader a number of different attitudes that I believe could have existed prior to the Civil War. It is also a story about a boy whose interest in learning leads him to ask numerous questions as he tries to make sense of the attitudes, events, and interests of others.

I would like to thank the rangers and Fort Sumter National Historic Site for sharing their knowledge and expertise with me in regard to life in Charleston, South Carolina, and the events leading up to one of the most significant periods in the history of the United States.

I would also like to thank my husband, Dale, who encouraged me to write this story.

CHAPTER 1

• • •

"WILL! DID YOU FEED THOSE chickens?"

"Yes, Pa. Just finished. Looks like we got some extra eggs today. Can I go to Market Street to sell 'em?"

"Not today. Old Joshua is comin' today to mend the roof on the cabin. I think he'll need our help."

Pa and I don't got no slaves like lots of people around here, so we do the work ourselves except when Old Joshua gives us a hand. Joshua is an old black man. He used to be a slave. He told me his owner was good enough to let him work and buy his freedom, so he is what they call a freedman. He's been free for a time. He told me that when he got his freedom, he started working hard so he could buy his wife's freedom, too. He almost had enough saved up, but his wife died. He's been alone ever since.

Sometimes Pa has some money to pay him. Sometimes we have an extra chicken. Sometimes all we can do is cook up a big pot of stew, and Joshua will eat like he ain't et in days. Maybe he hasn't. He's a good friend to Pa and me. He might be one of the reasons we don't have slaves.

Pa says the government says that all men are created equal. He also says that God created man in his own image. Pa figures that's two good reasons not to own slaves. Besides, I can't imagine owning somebody like Old Joshua like we own a cow. Don't seem right. But lots of people here own slaves and have for a real long time, so that's just how it is.

I'm Will McShane, and I just turned eleven. Me and Pa—his name is John— live just outside of Charleston on the Cooper River. We got a little bit of a farm that my pa lived on all of his life, and my grandpa before that. Some McShane, a long time back, came here and worked real hard to get this land, and we've been on it ever since. It ain't a lot, but it's enough for us. We've got some chickens, a cow, and a few pigs. We go hunting and fishing whenever we want and can grow enough vegetables for us and sometimes have some left over to take to the market to sell for cash, but we grow as much cotton as we can. That's easy to sell in town at the docks. Then they load it on big boats and send it to other places.

I've been living with here with Pa my whole life, and except for Ma dying when Little Sarah was born, things are usually real quiet. And that was almost three years ago. But lately, everybody around is in a fuss about what's going on in Charleston, and I just don't know what it means. That's why I want to go to Market Street to sell the eggs. Sure, we can get some extra money, but I get to learn what's going on there.

"Here comes Joshua, son. While I go out back to get the ladder, you can put the eggs in the root cellar. This time of year, they'll stay cool 'til tomorrow, and I'll go to town with you. I'm thinking about taking a couple of the chickens so we can get some money for those new tools I been looking at. I want to get Little Sarah something special, too. It's almost her birthday." I hardly heard the last few words because he was walkin' away behind the cabin.

Little Sarah lives in the city in a big house with Aunt Fran. After Ma passed, Pa was scared that me and him couldn't take care of a little girl and the farm, so Aunt Fran said she would take the baby. She said it was the least she could do for Ma. Seems that Pa and Aunt Fran were real close growin' up. She's Pa's sister, and she said she felt like Ma was a sister to her. So Little Sarah lives in the big house with a rich family and even some slaves. Aunt Fran ain't rich. She works there for the family by watching over all the house slaves and planning parties and such.

"Be right back, Joshua!" I yelled to him on my way to the root cellar. I was back in a minute and asked, "What can I do? Pa says we're workin' on the roof."

"Hello, Will. Don't know yet what you can do. I gotta take a look. Before I do, I want you to have this. I made a little something for you and something for your sister." He held up two wooden figures that looked like people.

"These are something, Joshua! Did you carve these? Hey, Pa! Look what Joshua made for us. I got a soldier, and he made Sarah a little baby doll.

Joshua, how do you know how to do so many things? You can fix the roof, mend fences, take care of sick pigs, make toys, and lots of other stuff. Where'd you learn all of that?" I hadn't known him for very long, but sure was surprised at all the things he could do.

"Well, it started long time back when I was a boy, lots younger than you are. You knows I was a slave. We had to do lots of different things to keep the plantation working and the master happy. Ya learn quick when ya gotta in order to get your dinner, or not git whipped."

I had to ask. "Did you ever get whipped?"

"A few times." Joshua smiled at me. "Mostly when things was wrong, my pappy fixed 'em before the master knew. Later on, I got sold. It was terrible to leave my pappy and mammy, but it turned out good. That was the master that let me work and save some so as I could buy my freedom. The more I learned and the more jobs I could do, the faster I could get free. So that's what I did, and that's why I know so many different things."

"I wish I knew all those things. But I ain't been to school since Ma died."

"Ya ain't always got to be in school to learn. Ya watch and listen to what's going on. Pay 'tention to what's going on around you, and you'll learn plenty. Where's your Pa?"

Just then, Pa came from the other side of the cabin. "Mornin', Joshua. I been getting things ready so we can get to work."

"'Morning, Mister John. I's ready anytime."

"Pa," I said. "Look what he made for us. Ain't they fine?"

"Sure are. Thank you, Joshua."

"No need to thank me. Your boy is a good one. Your little girl is a pretty thing, too, and you's good to me. Let's take a look at the roof."

"I'm gonna help, too!" I said.

"Will," said Pa, "you hold the ladder 'til we get up, and hand us those tools."

"Then what can I do?"

"Iffin it's all right with your pa, how's about you go to the river and catch us a mess of catfish? I'll fry 'em up when we get this job done," said Joshua, looking at Pa a little scared-like.

"That's a darn good idea, Joshua," said Pa. "We ain't had any of your good cooking for a long time. You go ahead, boy. I know you would rather be fishing than here."

When I was getting my pole, I heard Pa tell Joshua that he didn't think he could ever make a good farmer out of me.

Joshua said, "Mister John, they's lots more things to do than farming. Once the boy learns, he'll be good at whatever he wants to do. He's good people, like you."

Pa was right. I'd rather be fishing or hunting than anything else I know. When I'm fishing, I can sit and think about all sorts of things. I try to guess where the water in the river is coming from and how many other people have been fishing in it. I try to think about where it might go after it goes past me. I know it goes to the ocean. I see that all the time when we go into the city. But I mean where it goes after that. What other land does it pass? What are the people like there? All that stuff. I don't know that I'll ever find out, 'cause I guess Pa thinks I should be a farmer.

Spike followed me to the river. He was a good dog to have around. When I wanted to hunt, he would help chase out the birds. When I wanted to sit and think, he would sit next to me like he was thinking, too. We weren't sure where Spike ever came from right after Ma passed. He just showed up, not much more than a pup then, and he decided that he had found himself a home. I know that there are some kinds of dogs that are special bred to do certain things, but I guess Spike was bred to do different stuff. He wasn't real big or real small. His coat was sort of shaggy, but not real long. He had lots of different colors all over. He looked like somebody splashed some paint and he got in the way. And he has short, pointy ears. That's why we call him Spike. He is good at watching the chickens and letting us know when a fox or weasel is looking for a meal in the pen. Wherever he came from, I'm glad he showed up. He is a good, quiet friend.

● ● ●

After I was fishing and thinking for some time, Old Joshua came up behind me and gave me a start so bad, I almost fell into the river. "How's dinner comin'?"

"Oh, Joshua, you gave me a fright. Guess I was thinking about something else."

"Guess you were. I watched you let a fish take your bait and get away. Do you have enough yet, or do you got to sit and think—I mean, fish—some more?"

"We could probably do with a couple more if I got more time," I said. "Besides, I don't mind sittin' and thinkin' a little more, too."

"What you picturin' in your head?"

"Well, Joshua, do you ever think about things you ain't seen? Things far away and people far away? How they talk and how they dress?"

"Ya know," started Joshua, "I seen a lot in my time. I seen a lot that I don't want to think about. I seen some other places, but they look most like this. I don't guess I want to see any more."

"I'd like to see lots more. Before Ma passed, she made me go to school. I used to try to get out of it, but she even argued with Pa that I should go. I ain't been to school since Little Sarah was born, and I'm starting to miss it. Pa says as long as I can read some and know my numbers, that's enough for a farmer. I suppose it is.

"But, Joshua, I remember the teacher talking about other places. Places far away. Places so cold that it was hard for people to live and they couldn't grow anything. They only had whales and reindeer to eat. She told about places that were so hot and dry nobody and almost nothing lived there 'cept some little critters.

"When we go to the city, sometimes Pa lets me go to the wharf and talk to the sailors. Some I can't understand them, and they don't know what I say. I want to know what is in the big crates they bring in. Where it's from and how they use it. I want to know where all this cotton goes that we send out there on those ships. I want to know a lot."

"That's a pretty tall order," he told me. "What do you think you goin' to do 'bout it?"

"Don't know. Haven't given that part much thought. Do you suppose Pa would let me go back to school after the crop is in?"

"Can't tell you that, Will. Guess you'll have to ask him to find out. Know what? They's lots more ways to learn things than school. You keep askin' questions and talkin' to people."

"Hey, another fish! A big one! We can go back so you can do your good cookin' for us!"

When we got back, Pa was cookin' up a pot of stew from the garden. We had a good crop of vegetables this year. "What's been keeping you two?" asked Pa.

Joshua looked at me and said, "Mister Will and me was talkin'." He only called me Mister Will when Pa was around. I guess that was from his days as a slave, 'cause I know Pa don't care, and I don't like it.

The fish that he cooked up was as tasty as ever and Pa said, "Joshua, I'm thankin' your ma or whoever taught you how to cook like this. It's somethin' special."

"I didn't get to spend much time with Mammy, but I got this and the basket makin' from her. The rest I learnt as I growed." He gave me a little smile and added, "I wonder if there ain't an easier way to learn lots more faster than it took me."

"Could be," said Pa. "But we are glad for all that you do know."

After we were done and had as much as we could eat, Joshua said it was time for him to go.

"Wait," said Pa. "I owe you for today."

"No, Mister John. Not today. Old Joshua had a real good day and don't need no more now. You take care, and don't ferget the extra coat of tar on the roof." With that, he was gone.

"Let's get this cleaned up, Will. We'll turn in early, 'cause it's gonna be a long day t'morra."

CHAPTER 2

• • •

"Get yourself up and moving!" I turned over and tried to ignore him, but Pa started shaking me. "We got chores to do before we head to town."

I think I said, "Yes, Pa." I'm not sure. But I did drag out of the bed to get my chores done and have some breakfast before we set out.

It didn't take too long, and by the time we were done, the sun was getting high and we could feel the heavy heat of morning starting to build.

We loaded up the things we were taking to the market on old Gray. She was the mare that helped us through planting, harvesting, and taking the cotton and vegetables into town. She'd been around as long as I could remember. She wasn't much to look at, but she never fussed and was gentle with me and Little Sarah.

We started the three-mile walk into town, and Spike started after us, barking and wagging his tail. Pa turned and spoke harsh. "Stay! You watch while we're gone. Keep the fox out of the chicken pen!" Spike sat down on the path like he knew what he was supposed to do.

"Good dog!" I shouted back at him. He got up, gave his tail a wag, and turned back toward the cabin.

Pa and me walked a ways being quiet, sort of enjoying the day before it got too hot and stuffy. I got to thinking about what Joshua had said the day before. It took me a while, but I worked up my courage to say, "Pa, how's about I go back to school? I would still do all my chores even if I had to get up before the sun, and I could still help you with everything you need. And I wouldn't go while we was picking the cotton, and I'd help you, and . . ."

"Hold up," Pa interrupted me. "What's this all about? School? Where did you get an idea like that? You don't need school to be a good farmer. I'll teach you whatever you need to know. You know how to read some, and you can do enough numbers that nobody will cheat you. What else do you need?"

"Pa, remember how Ma always said it was important to know about the world and learn about other people? I remember her saying that it helps you to get to know yourself."

"Boy, I loved your Ma. I still do. But she had some ideas that didn't always make sense."

"It ain't just what Ma said. I want to know. I want to know about those other places and other people. There are people that don't think like us, and if we know about 'em, we can know how to get along with 'em. I want to know about what's going on that makes us live like we live. Who decides how things get to be? If we don't learn about that, how can we decide how we want to be livin'?"

"Slow down, Will. Sounds to me like you been thinking about this a long time."

"Yes, sir."

"Well, then, if you been thinking that long and hard, I hope you'll give *me* some time to do some thinking."

"Yes, sir." I didn't say another word. He was at least thinking about it, and it was better than I had hoped for.

We walked on into the city and into the heat of the day.

• • •

Market Street is a place where there's always busy goings-on. All along the street are tables or carts with anything I could ever think of to sell or buy. Baskets of fruits and vegetables, chickens, pigs, butchered meat, fish, and made things, too. Ladies' bonnets and shoes and maybe a tray of breads or cakes. Tools, knives, guns, and sometimes a good huntin' hound.

Every time I go there, it sounds and smells different. Chickens cluckin' and roosters crowin', pigs squealin', dogs barkin', people talkin' and yellin' to get your attention to look at what they got to sell. Sometimes it smells like spices or sweets, sometimes like day-old fish, sometimes like fresh fruit. It's new each time.

All sorts of people are there, too. Most of the sellers are folks like us, bringin' extra of what we got to get a little money. Some of the sellers are there all the time, selling whatever they find. The folks that are interestin' are the ones buyin'. There are always a lot of slaves tryin' to find special things for their masters' parties or some fancy thing for the mistress. Sometimes the rich folk are lookin' around, telling a slave to do this or that or havin' the slave carry all the food they bought.

We worked our way into the crowd as far as we could and sold our vegetables and eggs right off of Gray. We didn't have enough this trip to bring the wagon. It didn't take long for some folks to notice the fresh eggs, and they were gone. While we were trying to sell the vegetables, Terrance came by with a sack.

Terrance is a slave. I think he's a little younger than me, and I know him good because he's owned by the Hawkins. They are the people that Aunt Fran works for. Terrance is pretty little, so he can't do much heavy stuff at the house. He usually has to muck out the stable, feed the horses, and run errands. "Hey, Terrance!" I shouted over the crowd. "Where you headed?"

"Can't stop and talk, Mr. Will. I's in a hurry to get some nails and tools from the smith that Master Hawkins ordered last week. Says if I dally today, he'll have my hide. Some furniture gots to get fixed, 'cause some 'portant folks is coming to some big election party." He was gone in a flash.

I wanted to ask him about the party, but just then, a young black girl started to ask me about the yams and beans. She bought most of what we had after some tough bargaining. She may have been young, but I could tell she had done this a lot of times before. "What are you getting all that for?" I asked, trying to see if I could convince her to buy the rest of what we had.

"Ain't so much for you to know, is it?"

"Just asking. Trying to be polite."

"Not that I need to tell you, but the missus is having a dinner so she and the ladies can have a place to talk about the election coming up. They're all in a fuss about it, and I heard her say that the menfolk won't let them say nothin' when they're around, so she and the ladies are going to talk without the men." Then she was gone.

We were lucky because we sold the rest of the carrots and collards and got a fair price. Seemed as if there were a lot of gatherings going on that needed more food. Pa and I walked through the rest of the market looking for something special for Sarah because it was close to her birthday. Pa's eyes landed on a pretty little hat with white flowers and pink ribbons. It was more money than he had wanted to spend, but he got it anyway. He gave me two pennies to get peppermint for Sarah and me. We almost always took her a peppermint as a treat when we went to see her.

I could see a small smile on his face when he looked at the hat while we were walking over to see Little Sarah and Aunt Fran. "Pretty hat, Pa," I told him.

"I know. Looks almost like the one your ma was wearing the first time I met her." Now I know why he spent the extra money.

Walking toward the end of Meeting Street, we saw lots of people in wagons that were full of lots of stuff. It was the time of year when the rich plantation owners started to move back into their mansions in the city for the winter. They called it "the season." Guess their "season" meant one party or gathering after another. I know that's when the market was the busiest. "Pa, do you know anything about the talk I heard from Terrance and the slave girl about election parties and such?"

"Well, son, what I know is that there's a Northerner running for president that nobody in the South seems to trust. They're saying that he wants to get rid of all the slaves."

"Will you vote for him, Pa? You don't like slavery."

"No, Will. There ain't no way I'd vote for this man Lincoln. You're right that I'm not fond of slavery and buying and selling people like horses, but think about it. What would life be like here if all of the slaves were set free at once? I don't think any whites would be safe. These folks have had their families torn apart, kept in chains, worked half to death, whipped, and who knows what all. Don't you think they might want to lash out at every white person they could find?"

"But, Pa, they wouldn't hurt us, 'cause we don't have slaves and don't want any."

"Do you think they all know that or care? Besides, what would happen to the farm if, all of a sudden, hundreds or thousands of slaves were set free without anything? No land, no belongings, no home. My guess is that they would take whatever they could get."

"That sounds pretty scary," I agreed. "No wonder you won't vote for him."

• • •

We walked on past the big houses and mansions that were between the market and the battery. The battery was at the end of Charleston that looked out into the harbor and had the Ashley River on one side and the Cooper River on the other. Charleston stuck out in the water like a thumb. There were cannons set up along the water to protect the city if an attack came from the harbor.

I was never too worried about any attack, because Fort Moultrie and Fort Johnson were on either side of the harbor, and they had been building a fort out at the end of the harbor right across from Fort Moultrie ever since before I was born. Nobody was ever sure if Fort Sumter would ever get done.

I couldn't figure out why they needed another fort in the middle. Castle Pinckney stood real close to the city on a little island. Maybe they were building 'cause Pinckney was pretty small and didn't look like it would do much good if some other country came in with big warships like I heard the British tried to do during the Revolutionary War. Couldn't think who would attack us now. There was always a lot of stuff sitting on the dock waiting to go out. Mostly lots of cotton, and maybe they thought pirates or somebody would try to steal it.

The Hawkins' house was right at the end of Meeting Street across from a park and the battery. This is where we were headed to see Sarah and Aunt Fran. Their house was one of the biggest ones, with a courtyard, stables, kitchen house, and some other outbuildings. The house was three stories and some more rooms above for the slaves to sleep. I'd been in the house a lot of times since Sarah had lived with Aunt Fran, but I'd never seen all of it. I tried to get a look at more of it each time I went, but Aunt Fran never let me out of her sight.

Pa and I got there as the bells on Saint Michael's Church chimed twice. We would have enough time to visit and play with Sarah and get back home before dark. The sun went down pretty early this time of year. "Pa," I said as we were walking up to the house, "how do so many people get so much money that they can get all of these big houses and gardens and things? It don't seem fair."

"Will, being fair ain't got nothing to do with it. Lots of these folks inherited plantations. Those are the folks that are moving into town now. They live and work on the plantation during the summer and come here for winter. I don't know why, 'cept so they can have parties with each other. Lots of the folks are merchants and made a lot of money shipping cotton and buying fancy stuff from Europe to sell to the rich folks. From what I know, that's how Mr. Hawkins got so rich. He's got some big cargo ships that are always going back and forth, filled with things that people will pay a lot of money for."

Pa stopped for a time and looked thoughtful. "Fair? I don't know, Will. I know we work hard but will never have a lot of things. From what I see, looks to me like some of these folks don't work at all but still have lots of money. So maybe it's not about what's fair. Maybe luck has something to do with it. One thing I know, I don't need a big fancy house and carriages. All I need is my land so's I have a place for you and Sarah when she gets a little older."

"I 'spect so. But it would sure be nice to be able to have somebody waitin' on us once in a while."

"Will, no need for envy. Even when people have a lot, there comes a time when it can come crashing down on 'em. We got what we need." His voice was getting a little louder, so I knew I better stop.

"Yes, sir." But I still wished in my head that I could go to one of those parties and have all the food cooked and served to me.

We tied Gray to the hitching post outside the house and went around to the servants' entrance. "Hey, Terrance. Did you get all the tools you needed to get?" I asked when I saw him in the garden tending the weeds.

"I did, Mr. Will, and Mr. Hawkins was real pleased I done it so quick. All's I gotta do now is get these pesky weeds out and I can have the rest of the afternoon to myself." Then, as a sort of afterthought he looked at Pa and said, "Afternoon, sir."

He seemed real excited about having some free time. I felt bad for him that he couldn't go fishin' of an afternoon or just sit and look at all the people going by. I was wonderin' how he managed to get time for himself, so I asked him. "Terrance, how is it you can get to have an afternoon? Don't slaves have to stay and work all day?"

"Guess some do, but Mr. Hawkins tells me chores to do, and if I do 'em fast enough, I can have the rest of the day so's I can do what I want. They's other slaves have to work all the day, but sometimes I can help out my mammy, or sometimes I go to the market and talk to folks." And then Terrance added, "Mr. Will, you can learn a lot from the folks there."

"I suppose you're right," said Pa. "Now can you go in and find Miss Fran for me, Terrance?"

"Yes, sir." He dropped the hoe and raced inside.

In a short time, he was back at his task, and Aunt Fran and Little Sarah came out of the house. "Papa! Willie!" shouted Sarah, who ran to hug Pa's leg. Didn't take long for him to have her up in his arms in a big hug. She clung around his neck for a time, then wiggled 'til he put her down and she was tugging at my hand. "Willy, candy. Go to the park." We all laughed while she pulled me toward the street.

"Go ahead, Will. I'll be right along. Fran, can you come sit with us for a while?"

Aunt Fran replied, "Just a few minutes, John. There's lots going on around here, with all the plantation folks getting back into the city. Mrs. Hawkins is fixing to have a big party in a few days. From what I hear, it's lots of folks trying to get somebody elected other than Lincoln."

"Why do they have to have a party to do that?" I asked while Sarah kept pulling at my pockets, looking for the peppermint stick she knew would be in there.

"I'm not real sure, Will. But from what I hear, they seem to think that if everybody votes for just one other candidate, somebody can beat Lincoln. There are three other people running for president. People are thinking they can get organized to vote for one of them, and then Lincoln couldn't free the slaves. That's all I know about it."

"Come on, Sarah. Let's run." Sarah squealed as we hurried across the street to the park that looked out over the harbor.

The park was surrounded by the battery. Most of the time things were quiet, but today there were cadets from the Citadel doing some sort of drill. It looked like they were pretending to load and fire the cannons. They looked real sharp in their uniforms. I watched 'em, wishing that someday I could go to a military school like the Citadel. It would be a chance to go off to war and see other places in the world.

While I was imagining, Sarah tugged at my hand and said, "Here comes Pa. What's that?" She was looking at the bonnet in his hand.

"Sarah," called Pa. "Come here." She ran to him, and he put the hat on her head, tying the pink ribbon under her chin. She looked real pretty when she ran back to me. "Look at me, Willie! Catch me!" and she ran across the grass.

I pretended to chase her for a time and then caught her. I picked her up and put her over my shoulder. She giggled and squirmed. I looked at Pa. He was watching her with a sad kind of smile.

After a time, we took Sarah back to the house. She cried a little, like she always did when we left, but Pa promised we would be back soon. We had to leave to get home before it got real dark.

CHAPTER 3

• • •

THE SUN WAS GOING DOWN, and it was getting a little cooler even though the air was still heavy. That's pretty much normal for early fall. Never cools down much until late October.

We seemed to be walking slower than usual. It was even slow for Gray. She was sort of pushing my hand as I led her. Pa was real quiet for a long time. I wanted to ask him about Sarah and when we could bring her home to live with us, but it didn't seem like a good time.

When we were getting close to home, Pa stopped. It took me a couple steps to realize he wasn't next to me. I stopped and turned to see what the problem was. Pa was looking at me real serious. "Will, I been thinking. If you really want to go to school, maybe we can work something out."

I was shocked but happy. "Yes, Pa, I'm sure we can!"

"You know that it isn't much of a school, and I would expect you to find out if Mrs. Wilson will still let you come and sit in. I would also expect that you would be around while we're picking the cotton and getting it into town to sell and to be around sometimes when I need you. What I'm saying, Will, is that it would be your responsibility to take care of the schooling and still do a lot of what you do now. I think I can get a little more help from Joshua, but he's getting pretty old and not so strong."

He said that all real fast, like he had planned it in his head. All I could think to say was, "Yes, sir." I was pretty surprised at it all.

"And besides," Pa went on, "your mother would have wanted you to get more schooling."

I knew now why he had been so quiet. He was thinking more about Ma than my going to school. I still missed Ma a lot, but I don't think I can even guess how much Pa missed her. "Pa, when do you think Sarah can come live with us?" I figured I might as well ask now.

"I wish it was today, Will. I don't think it will be for a long while. She has to be big enough so that somebody doesn't need to watch her every minute. She's a handful for Fran and the slaves at the Hawkins' place. There ain't no way we could get any work done and keep an eye on her, too."

I decided not to ask if Pa thought he would ever get married again. I wished he would so we could be a family, but I figured I'd asked enough for one day.

Pa was quiet again the rest of the way, but my mind was racing about school. He had been right about it not being much of one. The only reason it was there at all was because Mrs. Wilson had about ten young'uns and was from somewhere up north and thought that everybody needed to know how to read, including girls. There weren't but a few books that everybody shared, and there was a board that had black paint on it that we could write on and do numbers.

I would wait till tomorrow, but I was hoping that Pa would let me go and talk to Mrs. Wilson to see if I could start up again, with Pa's rules.

● ● ●

Pa did let me go the next day and even take Gray so I could get there and back faster. The "school" wasn't too far. The Wilson family lived about halfway between our place and town. They had cleaned out an old chicken coop and put some chairs and benches in it. Mrs. Wilson thought her children would learn better if there was a special place for it. Sometimes some of the youngsters from farms close by would come to learn to read. I heard tell that they would go home and teach their parents.

Most people didn't put too much stock in reading and numbers, so there was no real school for us. The folks in the city had special people they called tutors that came to their house to teach. I know that lots of the rich boys got to go to real schools far away. I would never be able to do that, but I might be able to do something else besides farming, though I wouldn't never tell that to Pa.

When I got to their place, it was all pretty quiet, so I figured they were all in the schoolroom. I stood outside the door for a minute and listened. One of the little ones was reading to the rest of them. It was something about a man named Paul Revere and red coats. I sure didn't know why red coats were important, but the reading was good. I knocked.

The reading stopped, and Mrs. Wilson opened the door. Mrs. Wilson was a nice lady but she talked a little funny, and sometimes it was hard to understand her. Ma had said that it was because she was from New York. "Hello. Aren't you young William? I haven't seen you in quite a while."

"Yes'm," I replied and hung my head a bit. "Sorry to interrupt your school, but I was wondering if I could maybe come back sometimes to learn more readin'."

"Well, that sounds like a good idea, but I will have to think about it. With the big family and all, I don't have a lot of extra time."

"I'd be willing to help out some so's you would have the time." I blurted that out without thinking about all I had promised Pa. But I wanted to go back to school and would do almost anything.

Mrs. Wilson thought for a moment and then looked at the other children. "Well, what do you think?" she asked them and then added, "what if we asked William to clean up the classroom after we were done? Then you children could get to your chores sooner." They all looked at each other and nodded and said yes, almost at the same time. I guess nobody liked to take care of the classroom. "It wouldn't be a big job," Mrs. Wilson told me. "It would mean sweeping, cleaning off the writing board, and getting water in the pail so we could start the next day."

"It don't seem like much," I said. "Are you sure that's all?"

"Yes, William. It will help us, and I know you have to help your father on the farm. With all of that and studying, that will keep you busy."

"Oh, Mrs. Wilson, speaking of Pa, I promised him I'd help when the cotton is ready. That should be in a couple of weeks, and I won't be able to be here at all."

"That's all right. You come when you can. I'm sure you must really want to learn, so I will help you as much as I can. I would also expect you to help out with the smaller children and the new student."

"Yes, ma'am." Then I stuttered, "N-new student? Who is that?"

"His name is James O'Rourke. He and his family just moved here from Pennsylvania. They had to move in with his father's family because of an illness, and his mother wants him to be able to continue studying as much as possible. He will be helping out here when we need him to, also. I'm not so concerned about how much you boys do, but rather that you understand that if you want something, it is important to work for it."

"Yes, ma'am. I'll go so you can keep teaching, but I'll be back tomorrow. Is it OK if I bring the book Ma had? Maybe I could learn to read all the big words."

"Certainly, William. The more books we have, the more ideas we learn. What is it?"

"Something about George Washington. I'll see you tomorrow."

I heard Charles from the other side of the room say, "Bye, Will." I guess he remembered me from the times I saw his family at church. I said good-bye and closed the door as Mrs. Wilson told me I should be there early in the morning.

I took a deep breath and almost laughed out loud. I was going back to school again! I guess I would be real busy.

I hurried home and told Pa what had happened and about the new boy. He said he hoped I hadn't taken on too much, but if I could keep up, that would be fine. Then he said, "I think I know who Mrs. Wilson is talking about. Do you remember the O'Rourkes?"

"Aren't they the old people that live up the road two or three miles?"

"They only had one son: Thomas. He joined up with the army when there was talk of war with Mexico. I remember that they were real sad to see him go. I heard he was stationed someplace in the North—maybe it was Pennsylvania—met a gal, married, and got a job in the coal mine after the war. Can't guess why he came back, except maybe to help out his folks."

"Mrs. Wilson said something about an illness. Don't know who is sick, but I suppose I'll be finding out tomorrow."

• • •

The next morning I was up earlier than usual. It was just starting to lighten. I figured I'd do a good job on my chores before I left and still be at the Wilsons' early. By the time the chickens were fed, eggs collected, and the cow was milked, I was already in a sweat. It was cool, but the air was thick with haze. It's always like that around this time of year. Nights start cooling down, and then, for some reason, you can almost see the water in the air.

I went in for some breakfast before I left. I broke off a piece of bread from the loaf and dipped it in the fresh milk. It was real sweet. I asked Pa if he wanted me to fry up some eggs for us. "Good idea, Will. Put a few extra in the pan. Old Joshua will be coming around to help with the fence today." He and Pa were building a sturdy corral for Gray and the cow for winter. The old one got knocked down in a bad storm at the end of summer. We were lucky, though, because the tree that broke it apart didn't hit the shed or cabin.

"Is it right that I'm going, Pa? I don't want to have somebody else doing my work." I was wondering now if I did the right thing.

"It's fine, son. We'll give it a try. If it don't work out, we'll change something."

"Thanks, Pa." I was relieved. Then I added, "Do you guess Ma knows from heaven?"

"I'm sure she does, Will. And I'm sure she would be happy about it. Now, stop jabbering and get those eggs cooked and get yourself to school!"

"Hey, Pa. You know you sound a little like Ma?"

He smiled and set the table for three.

I had eaten and was on my way down the road with Ma's book under my arm when I met Joshua. "Joshua!" I shouted. "I'm going to school! Ain't that great?"

"Yes, siree! You listen to me, Will. I'm gonna help your Pa as much as I can so's you can have more time to study and learn those things you want to learn. You can't never know too much. Learning must be important, 'cause the white folks never wanted us Negros to read or learn nothing. That way all the slaves would have to depend on them. You learn lots, and you don't have to depend on nobody else."

"I gotta run to not be late!" I wondered what he had meant about not depending on anybody else and learning, but I forgot about it when I opened the door and went into school.

The young'uns were finishing up their chores and coming into the school the same time I got there. I saw another boy about my age. I figured that was who Mrs. Wilson had told me about. I sat next to him on the bench and introduced myself. "Hey, my name is Will. You must be James."

"Jimmy. Mrs. Wilson is the only one that calls me James. I don't hardly know who she's talking to sometimes." I smiled and told him that she also called me William. Jimmy nodded. He looked at the book I had brought in. "That looks like a big book," he said. "Did you read it all?"

"No, not yet. It was my ma's. Mrs. Wilson said she'd help me with it."

"Doesn't your ma want it anymore?" he asked.

"She died."

"Oh." That was all he said for a time and looked at the floor. "That's got to be real hard. I can't imagine what it would be like without one of my parents. I'm hoping I don't have to find out. Pa's been sort of sick for a long time. That's one of the reasons we moved here."

I tried not to be rude, but I was curious. "What's the matter with him?"

"The doctor back home thought it had something to do with coal mining."

Just as I was going to ask what he meant about that, Mrs. Wilson walked in, straightening her apron. She announced that we were going to get started. "I see you two have gotten to know one another. You'll have more time for talking later. Now we will start with our numbers. Elizabeth, please go to the writing board and write the multiplication table for the number two. Then we will all repeat them."

We spent the morning on two times everything until we knew them all. Then we shared the books to do some reading, and Mrs. Wilson asked me if I would read the first page of the George Washington book. I told her I didn't think I knew all the words, but she helped, and everybody learned something about the first president.

Seemed like it wasn't very long before she said we were done for the day. I should stay and straighten up the room, and Jimmy should follow Charles to the barn to clean out the horse stall. Our work didn't take either of us very long and we were on our way home. We could walk together for a ways before the road forked and he went off the other way.

We didn't talk much at first, but I asked him if he liked to go fishing. He said he'd like it fine. Just about at the same time, we both said that we should go tomorrow after school. He would ask his ma, and I would check with Pa to see if it was all right. Then he got real serious and asked, "What's it like without your mother?"

That surprised me. After a minute, I said, "Guess I hadn't thought about it much, 'cause that's just the way it is. Some things are different than I remember. We don't get good pies and cakes anymore, just sometimes from the city if Pa thinks we got a little extra money, but they ain't like I remember Ma making. The hardest thing is that Little Sarah can't live with us."

"Who's that?"

"She's my little sister. That's when Ma died. She lives with my Aunt Fran in the city in one of the mansions where my aunt works. No way we could take care of a baby and the farm, so we're lucky she's so close." I stopped for a minute and said, "Guess the worst thing is that I miss Ma awful. It ain't so bad now like it used to be, but I remember how she looked and the way she laughed." Jimmy didn't say a word. I don't know if he was thinking or didn't know what to say, so I added, "Pa and me are doing good, and we get to see Sarah, so I guess it will work out fine."

We came to the fork in the road. "I have to turn here. I'll see you tomorrow, Will." He walked away pretty slow with his head down, like he was thinking. I wondered if he was thinking about his pa. I would remind myself tomorrow to ask about how coal minin' could make you so sick you could die.

CHAPTER 4

• • •

"I'm home, Pa!" I shouted as I came close to the cabin. Pa came around from the back of the house. He had been in the garden and had his hands full of collards and yams.

"All right, boy. Go have something to eat. Take these in with you. Hurry on and come out and help me finish off the fence. Joshua left a while ago. I told him to go on home and rest. He looked terrible tired."

While we were finishing the fence, Pa told me that Joshua had taken a fall from a ladder while he was helping the Widow Caldwell 'cause her son hurt his arm. Pa guessed maybe Joshua had hurt his back and was in a lot of pain. Pa tried to get him to rest in the cabin, but he wouldn't, so Pa told him to go and not come back until he felt better. "I told him he was a lot of help to a lot of people, but that he would be no good to nobody if he was hurtin'."

I was thinking I should stay here tomorrow when Pa said, "Will, after we do this, I want you to get the can of milk out and churn it to butter. We've got enough, and it will go bad if we don't use it. Then tomorrow after school, you are to take the butter to your Aunt Fran. I told her that I would send some as soon as we got it churned. She said it was hard to keep up with everything, what with all the commotion about the election coming up and everybody in the city in a frenzy."

I thought about going fishing with Jimmy, and I hated churning. It took forever, like you were going to always just move the paddle up and down. There were a few things that confused me about the election and why Aunt Fran needed our butter. So I said, "Pa, why does she need our butter? She could easy get some at the market."

"Boy, I told her we would do it. She takes care of your sister, and she don't complain. Are you going to complain because I asked you to help her out?"

"No, sir." I knew better than to mention the fishing I had hoped I could do, so I changed the subject. "What's the big goings-on about the election?"

"The closer the election comes, the more people are getting upset about Lincoln. They got all sorts of parties going on so somebody like Breckinridge will get elected and they don't have to worry about anybody taking away the slaves."

"When is the election, Pa?"

"First week in November. Only a couple of weeks from now. I hope things settle down soon. Seems like everybody is jittery."

I finished the churning after what seemed like days. I truly hated doing it.

After we had some supper, I asked Pa if I could light the lamp. We didn't use it much, because oil was expensive. It had been one of the few things of Ma's that Pa had kept. "What do you need that for?" he asked.

"I want to do some reading in the book. I'm working out the words, and Mrs. Wilson said she'd help me. I read some at school today. It's about George Washington. I think he was a good man even before he was president, and I want…"

"Hold on, Will. Take a breath. You seem pretty excited about all this." He stopped for a minute and smiled. "It would've made your Ma proud. We don't have enough oil for the lamp, but there are some small candle pieces. I saw 'em on the shelf behind the big stewpot. If you're gonna keep readin', why don't you ask Aunt Fran if they got candle ends they can't use no more?"

"Thanks, Pa." I lit the candle stub and sat down to work on the words on the next pages. After a time, my eyes started getting heavy, and the light was about gone. I guessed that would be the end of my day.

• • •

The next morning, after I did what needed to be done, Pa said, "Make sure you take some bread and a piece of salt pork so you can eat it on the way to town. I don't want you to dally none. It gets dark early."

"I know, sir. I won't."

"But," Pa continued, "I do want you to spend a little time with Sarah, and I want you to stop by and look in on Old Joshua. Do you remember where-abouts he calls home?"

"I think so. Ain't it in one of those shacks by the dock?"

"That was the last place I know of. He may have moved on. But try to find him and see how he's doing and if we can help him somehow." I didn't know what we could do to help, but if Pa said so, I'd do it. He went on, "Depending on when you get back, I may not be here."

I was surprised. "Where would you be?"

"I'm going over to see about the Caldwells. They may need some help with the oldest boy being hurt. Thought I'd give them a hand if they need it before we start picking the cotton. Oh, Will, tell Mrs. Wilson you won't be there for a while after the next few days. We can start picking anytime."

"Yes, Pa. Can I start tomorrow after school?" I figured the more I could get done after school, the more days I would be able to go.

"Any time, boy. As long as it ain't raining. You better get going, and don't forget the butter. Put some of the extra eggs in that bucket and give 'em to Mrs. Wilson. I 'spect with all those young'uns, they could use a few."

"Thank you, Pa. I feel like it helps me pay for what she's doing for me."

"Son, neighbors and friends don't need no pay. We get a few extra, and they can use 'em. That's all. Now, go."

• • •

When I got to the fork in the road, I saw that Jimmy was there, a ways ahead, so I shouted to him. He stopped and turned and waited. I saw a package under his arm. "I got bad news," was the way he greeted me. "Can't go fishing today. I've got to go to town. Ma did some sewing for Mrs. Hawkins in the city and promised her she would get it there by today, so I lose out. I hate going alone, because I've only been there one other time and I'm afraid I won't find it."

I sort of chuckled inside and looked at him serious. "I got more bad news, Jimmy. I gotta take this pail of butter to my aunt who works at the Hawkins' place, and I've been there lots of times. I know where it is. I guess we should go together if'n you can do another errand with me on the way."

"You bet!" He smiled and sounded relieved.

We started walking faster when I asked him about coal mining and how it can make a person sick. "Lots of coal miners were getting sick, and folks were saying it was from breathing in coal dust. Pa took to coughing so bad, sometimes he would cough up blood and could hardly breathe. Ma said he wasn't going into the mine any more. I thought I'd be going to work there. There's lots of boys my age in the mine. They can get into small places."

I shuddered to think about being stuck in a dark hole all day.

"Ma said she'd have no son of hers go down there. So there was nothing else to do but come here to help with Pa's folks and hope he got better."

"Is he getting better?"

"I think some. He doesn't cough so bad now, but it's hard for him to breathe, so he can't do hard work. I think I should be helping Grampa more, but Ma says I have to go to school while I can."

We finished our walk in silence and went into school. The morning seemed to go by fast. We all repeated the numbers times three, practiced some reading, looked at a map of the United States, and the time was up.

Jimmy and I did our few small chores and started toward town when I remembered the eggs. "Be right back," I said to Jimmy over my shoulder. "Mrs. Wilson! I forgot something."

She met me at the path to the house. "My goodness, William. What's wrong?"

"Nothing, ma'am. Almost forgot to give you these eggs Pa sent and tell you we'd be picking cotton soon, so I'd be missing some school."

"Well, bless him. It's like he knew the fox got another one of the chickens last night. Thank you, William, and thank your father for me."

"You need a dog like our Spike."

"I guess we do."

We were almost to town when Jimmy asked what the extra errand was. I told him about Joshua and that we would go past the docks to try to find his shack. "You know Old Joshua?"

Jimmy looked worried. "I heard of him. Grampa said he came around once looking for work, but Grampa told him he wouldn't pay a slave to do work. Can't let Grampa find out I been looking for a slave."

"He ain't a slave. He's free." I knew there were people that hated slaves just because they were black.

"I know," said Jimmy, "and where I come from, lots of people hate slavery and are hoping if Lincoln gets to be president, he can stop it from spreading to other states."

"If Lincoln gets to be president, he's going to end slavery, and we'll all be hurtin' from it," I argued.

"That's not the way I heard it. Ma and me read in a newspaper back home that Lincoln said in front of a big crowd of people that slavery shouldn't be allowed to spread, but that he knew there was nothing he could do to stop it where it was already."

I thought about that for a while. I began to wonder if Pa didn't know about what was in that newspaper and maybe he just heard it all from other people who didn't know about the newspaper. "Well, I don't know about any of that, but nobody around here wants the slaves to be free."

• • •

When we got to the row of shacks, there was a black man sitting on a crate. I asked him if he knew Joshua and where he might be. The black man looked at me funny and nodded down the row. "Next one down," was all he said and watched us as we knocked on the door and went in.

It was dark and took a minute for our eyes to be able to see. The first thing I noticed was the smell. It was like the place had never been clean. When I could see, there wasn't much to look at—just some crates and a board for a table. Joshua was laying on the floor on a blanket.

"What are you doin' here, Will? You should be at school or home helping your Pa. And who is this?" asked Joshua after he caught sight of Jimmy. I was surprised he didn't get up.

"This is my friend Jimmy. I *am* helping Pa. He told me to come by and see how you was doing and if there was anything we could help you with."

"Hello, Jimmy. Sorry I ain't getting up to welcome you, but this old back ain't working right today, and it's a lot less aggravatin' if I lay down. Will, you tell your Pa thank you for looking in, but I'll be good as new in a few days. Shouldn't need help, just some healin' time. Clumsy old man, that's me."

I smiled and was about to turn to leave when I asked, "You got any food here?"

"I'll be getting me some as soon as I get this old bag o' bones off the floor."

I took the bread and pork out of the pail, gave it to him, and said, "Almost forgot! Pa sent this for you."

"Thanks, Will. That was right thoughtful. You and your Pa are good people, and I'm gonna remember that wherever I am."

"What do you mean, wherever you are?"

"Just been thinking that maybe Sadie is waitin' for me and be coming to get me pretty soon."

"Joshua"—I used the kind of voice Pa used with me when he was going to say something important—"You listen to me! You stop talking like that. Sadie will be waitin' forever. So you just get well, and you can go see her later. You hear me?"

"Yes, Masah Will." He chuckled when he said it. I knew he was teasing me, but it was sad to me that he could still think like a slave.

"Pa and me will be looking to see you as soon as you're better."

As we walked out, Jimmy asked, "Who's Sadie?"

"That was his wife that died as a slave a long time ago," I said, and then I was quiet the rest of the way to the Hawkins'. Jimmy shared his bread and jerky with me on the way. I guess Pa was right about friends.

• • •

Aunt Fran was in the kitchen and opened the door as soon as we got there. "Hey, Aunt Fran. I got your butter here."

"Thanks, Will. Even a little less to do around here lately is a help. Who's this?"

"This is Jimmy. He's new here. He's from Pennsylvania."

"Pennsylvania? That must be interesting, coming from the North. I'm sure you must be learning a lot."

"Yes'm," Jimmy mumbled. He took the package from under his arm and handed it to Aunt Fran. "This is the sewing Ma did for Mrs. Hawkins."

"Oh, yes. Mrs. Hawkins mentioned someone would bring it today. She gave me this for your mother." Aunt Fran handed Jimmy a coin and said, "Be careful not to lose it."

"No, ma'am."

"Where's Sarah?" I asked, looking around the kitchen. She was often there with my aunt.

"Sarah is at the park with Annie."

"Who is Annie?" I thought I knew the names of all the Hawkins folks and their servants and didn't remember Annie.

"Miss Annie Davis. She has just come here from New York. It seems her folks thought she should go to the ladies' finishing school here in Charleston. Her father and Mr. Hawkins know each other from business they do up north. When Mr. Davis asked Mr. Hawkins if he knew of a place a young lady could live while she went to school, Mr. Hawkins said that they had plenty of room and she would be safe here. It's real convenient for them too because her brother is a soldier at Fort Moultrie on Sullivan's Island. He's here with her and Sarah now across in the park."

Jimmy and I walked across the street, eating big ginger snaps that Aunt Fran gave us. We were both still hungry after our shared lunch. As soon as Little Sarah spotted me, she came running with Miss Annie and a soldier right behind her. The soldier scooped her up so she couldn't get away, but she wiggled and squirmed and cried until he put her down, and she ran toward us again.

I got down on my knees so I could give her a big hug, and the soldier was right over me. He had on a blue uniform with brass buttons and a belt with a sword hanging from it. It had me scared. "Boy, what are you doing with that little girl? Leave her alone and get away from here!"

I stammered, "My name is Will McShane, and this little one is my sister, sir."

The soldier looked at Miss Annie. She was pretty, with curls all over her head and a nice smile. She looked at the soldier and said, "He certainly could be her brother. Miss Fran told me about him and his father and why Sarah lives in Charleston instead of on their farm."

Sarah was smiling big and squealed, "Willie, where's Pa?"

"He couldn't come today, Sarah. But he sent me and my friend Jimmy to see you. He said he would come real soon. We'll be bringing some cotton to town in a few days." I said that more to the others, because Sarah wouldn't really know what that was all about.

"Where are my manners? I'm Annie Davis, and this is my brother, Lieutenant Jefferson Davis. I've just come here from New York to go to school while Jeff is at Fort Moultrie."

"I'm Will, and this is Jimmy. Nice to meet you, ma'am." I was glad I remembered some of my manners. Her brother still scared me.

"Well," said the lieutenant. "I can see you are in good company now, Annie. I must be getting back to the fort to report to Colonel Gardner about the supplies and his replacement. It was nice to meet you boys. I hope I didn't startle you, but I was afraid Sarah was running away from us."

"Yes, sir," was all I could sputter. Jimmy nodded.

"Will, are you and Jimmy going to be here for a while to play with Sarah? It looks like she would love to be with you. I'll go back to the house if you will bring her back to Miss Fran before you leave. I need to attend to my studies."

"We can't stay very long, but 'course I'll bring her back."

Before we left, I asked Aunt Fran about the candles, and she loaded the pail with lots of part-burned candles. "We always have a supply of them, even after the servants take what they need. You can have all you want. But what do you need them for?"

"Reading," I announced proudly. I'm going to school again, and 'cause the sun goes down so early now, I gotta have some light."

"Good for you, Will. Your ma would be proud of you. Speaking of the sun going down early, you'd better be heading on home."

CHAPTER 5

• • •

"Wow! I never saw a soldier with so much brass." Jimmy was very impressed with Lt. Davis.

"Do they have to get dressed up like that all the time, or just when they go out for special meetings?" I figured Jimmy knew more about it than I did because his father had been a soldier. I had seen the Citadel cadets in uniform a lot of times, but I was like Jimmy—had never seen so much brass.

"I think mostly for special stuff when they want to look good."

"He sure looked good," I said. "Maybe I should be a soldier and then I could travel all over and learn about other places."

"Well, my father was a soldier and I don't think he liked it much. He got to see some places in Texas and Mexico but doesn't talk about it a lot. I remember him saying once how bad it all was when everybody was shooting at everybody else."

I hadn't thought about that part. Maybe it wasn't such a good idea.

We split up at the fork in the road, and I hurried on because the sun was beginning to get low and Pa would be worried. As I got close to the cabin, Spike came trotting out to me wagging his shaggy tail. "Hey, Spike. Good dog. Where's Pa?"

Since Spike wouldn't answer, I called out for Pa, but there was no answer there, either. I was glad he had told me he was going to the Caldwells' so that I wouldn't have to worry.

I was just opening the door when he called out from behind me. "Will, hold that door open. I don't want to dump this pie!"

"Pie! Sure will, Pa. We ain't had pie in a long time."

"Well, we got one now. Mrs. Caldwell made us a sweet-potato pie." I started to think that we should go help her more often.

"How's Dirk?" I knew he was the oldest Caldwell and guessed he was the one that got hurt.

"Healing fine, but they needed a few things done that he couldn't manage with a bad arm. I think they'll be able to get the cotton picked, but we may have to help get it into town. Speaking of cotton, I think we need to get started tomorrow and hope we can get a load in early. Sometimes there's a better price if it's the first in."

"Yes, Pa. I thought I'd start after school."

"No, son. We'll start early and work all day. I told you, school would have to wait when it was time. And I think it is time."

"Yes, sir." I knew this would happen, but hoped it would be later. I promised myself I would pick as fast as a person could so we could get finished sooner.

We finished our supper with a lot of the best sweet-potato pie I think I ever had. I told him about Sarah, Miss Annie, and Lt. Davis and his fancy uniform. Pa nodded and said that he was glad that Sarah and Miss Annie got along. I lit a candle and did some reading. I wanted to keep working on that book, even if I wasn't in school.

● ● ●

I hurried to finish the regular chores in the morning so I could start picking the puffy white cotton. It looked easy enough, but it didn't take long for my fingers to get sore from all the seeds in the cotton boll that are real sharp.

Late in the afternoon, when our backs were hurtin' so bad, we didn't think we could move, Pa said we should quit for the day and go sit at the river and catch some dinner. We had done a lot of work that day, and he said he thought we deserved a break.

While we were waiting for something to bite, Pa said, "Will, I forgot to ask you about Joshua. Did you find him yesterday? How is he?"

"I found him, all right, but I don't know how he was. He couldn't get off the floor, he hurt so bad. It was pretty dark in the shack, so I couldn't see how he looked, but he didn't sound good. Pa, he didn't have no food."

"I 'spect somebody will help him out. The folks that live around there take care of their own. We'll be going to town in a few days as soon as we get a wagonload of cotton. We'll take him some food and check on him then. Hey, watch the pole! I think you have dinner on the hook."

I pulled up a big one and Spike started to bark. Guess he figured he'd have some of the fish, too.

After we cooked up the fish and finished off the pie, I lit the candle again, figuring I'd do some reading. All of a sudden I felt Pa shake me. I wasn't sure how long I had been sleeping. "Will, you can't read with your head on the book. Off to bed. Reading will have to wait."

• • •

The next few days were real busy. We got a lot of the cotton picked, but I couldn't get much reading done. I was way too tired by the time we finished supper.

When we had a wagonload, it was time to take it into town to sell. There was more left that needed to be picked, but we could only take a one load at a time. I always liked to go into the city to sell it because that's when we would have some extra money for things we needed and sometimes a little for some special things. I'd seen some map books at the market once, and I hoped maybe I could buy one to look at all the places I wanted to go.

Pa thought that if we got the cotton in early, we might get a better price. We got nine cents a pound last year, and he was hoping for ten or more this time. We hooked up Gray to the wagon, packed up some extra eggs and a pail of milk for Joshua, and we were on our way. We didn't say much on the way in. I liked feeling the cooler weather, especially this early in the morning. The end of October is one of my favorite times.

When we were getting close, I asked Pa if we were going to stop to see about Joshua first.

"No, we'll take care of the cotton, and then come back before we go to see Sarah."

We weren't the first at the dealer but didn't have to wait long before we could get the cotton unloaded and weighed. "Nine and a half cents a pound, McShane, and you got three hundred pounds." The dealer was gruff and all business.

"Thought maybe the price would go up this year," said Pa. "You sure it's only three hundred?"

"Price did go up. It was only nine cents last year. You got a problem with my scales, then you weigh it someplace else and move on."

I think Pa would have liked to take it someplace else, but since it was unloaded already, he just nodded. The dealer handed him the money and moved to the next wagon. "Well," Pa said as we walked away, "I was hoping for better than that, but I guess we gotta take what we can get since we don't have to clean or bale it. I hear some of the big planters get twelve cents a pound, but they got the cotton gins and slaves to do the work."

I guessed that seemed fair, but it didn't seem like we could ever compete and get equal pay.

"Come on, Will. Let's go see Joshua. And I want to stop at the blacksmith to see if he can fix the harness now that I've got the money to pay him. Then we'll go see Sarah."

"Pa, can we stop at the market to get some peppermint for Sarah and maybe look at some of those map books I seen last time we were here?"

"Peppermint, yes. No books until all the cotton is in and we see what we have."

"But can I just look, Pa?"

"Not now, boy." Pa used the voice that meant I didn't need to ask again.

As we came to the shacks, the same man was sitting on the same crate I had seen when I was here before. "Remember me? I was here looking for Joshua a few days ago."

"I 'member, young sir," he answered but never looked at Pa or me directly.

"We came back to see him and bring him something to eat."

"Well, sir. Joshua won't be needin' anything to eat."

"Why not? Did he go away? Pa, he wouldn't leave without telling us!"

Pa was quiet, and the old man went on. "He didn't tell nobody. He gone, but he gone to be with the Lord and Sadie."

"No! He said he was fine and he would be up in a few days." I swallowed hard and tried not to believe what the man had told us, but I knew Joshua was dead. Pa put his arm around me. When I looked up at him, I could see him swallow hard, too.

"Will, we have to accept it." Then he asked the black man, "Where is he buried?"

"Don' know. I tol' the constable Joshua dead, and they come with a wagon and take him away."

"You don't know!" I shouted. "Where is he buried? When was the funeral? Who was the pastor who said some prayers?" I had remembered that from Ma's funeral.

"Ain't no funeral, ain't no pastor. I said a prayer to the Lord and to Sadie when they take him away. Don' know where they bury black folks."

"That's wrong! No funeral? Like nobody cared if he lived or died? How can they do that? Pa, where would they take him?"

"There's special cemeteries for black folks, Will. When nobody takes care of the body, they put it in what they call a pauper's grave. I don't think we'll ever find it."

"It ain't right, Pa. Joshua was a good man. He should have had somebody there to pray over him like they did with Ma. It ain't right!"

"May not be right, son, but that's the way it is. I know you feel bad, and so do I, but there ain't much we can do. Let's get on to the market for that candy."

As we were walking to the market, I couldn't help thinking how bad it would be to be treated like that. "Pa, why do they treat black people like they ain't even people? They have a right to be buried like anybody else."

"Black people got no rights, Will." He stopped and turned me to face him. "You listen to me. We will not talk about black folks' rights here in the city. People hear you talking like that, and bad things can happen. We'll talk about it at home. You hear me?"

"Yes, sir. But what bad things?"

"At home. Not another word about it 'til then."

I swallowed hard again. I didn't understand how a good man could disappear from the earth with nobody taking notice. It didn't seem right.

We didn't say a word all the way to the Hawkins' house. When we got there, Aunt Fran told us that Sarah was across the street with Miss Annie. She also told us not to go home without the bread she had just baked and some more candles she had collected. I wasn't about to leave without her bread! "How's the book going, Will?"

"I ain't had time to read much 'cause of the cotton. I'm hoping I can get back to school next week some," I told her as I looked at Pa.

He gave me a nod and said, "Let's go see Sarah. Oh, no! We forgot to get her a peppermint. I guess we had other things on our minds."

Sarah was playing with Miss Annie. She ran to Pa and me as soon as she saw us. Miss Annie started after her until she recognized me, and then she smiled. "Hello, Will. Is this your father?"

"Yes. Miss Annie, this is John McShane," I said, remembering my manners.

"It's nice to meet you, Mr. McShane."

"Nice meeting you, miss. Will said you just moved here. How do you like Charleston?"

"I really am enjoying it. I like the weather much better than New York, and the people have been very welcoming and courteous. I've learned a lot as well."

"You mean because you're going to school." I thought that would help to convince Pa.

"Yes, Will. Of course, I'm learning a lot at school, but I'm also learning about the different kind of life people here live. One of the things that surprised me was about slavery. To hear people in the North talk, you'd think that everyone here beat and starved their slaves. The people I have met have really been kind to their servants. Mind you, I don't agree with the institution of slavery, but here it doesn't seem as awful as I have heard. Well, I've talked too much. I'll leave you with Sarah. It was nice to see you again, Will. Mr. McShane." She held her hand out to shake Pa's.

He was a little surprised but took her hand and nodded. "Miss Annie."
She turned and walked away.

Pa took a breath. "Well, she's an interesting young woman."

I think he meant it in a good way. She was sure different than a lot of
Southern ladies who never seem to say much about things other than parties,
and they sure never shake a man's hand. Guess that's another good reason
to travel and learn about how other people do things. But I don't think she
learned how bad slavery could be.

We played with Sarah for a time, and then took her back across the street,
got Aunt Fran's fresh bread, and started home.

When we were well out of town, I asked Pa why it was so awful to say
stuff about black people having a decent burial. "Will, a lot of folks don't understand that you just want to be nice to people. They hear you talking, and
they think you want slaves to be free and live like us. Some of those folks can
get pretty mean. I heard tell that some crops got burned and livestock killed
at a farm where some hotheads got the idea those folks wanted Lincoln to be
elected. With the election in about a week, you have to be careful what you
say. People are edgy."

"Yes, Pa. I understand." I really didn't, but knew I had better keep quiet.

That night, I couldn't concentrate on reading. I picked up the soldier that
Joshua had carved for me. I couldn't swallow hard enough. I cried.

CHAPTER 6

• • •

PA LET ME GO TO school the next two days, but I had to hurry home and help finish picking the cotton. We figured we'd be done early next week if it didn't rain. I was even able to get some reading done since the sun was setting earlier so we had to stop, and I had more time after supper.

Tuesday morning, Pa said I couldn't go to school. We were going to finish picking and get it all into town by Wednesday. We'd take some time at the market to get supplies before we went to see Aunt Fran and Little Sarah. It was a lot of hard work, but I was glad when Wednesday morning came and the wagon was loaded. We walked as fast as we could, because we had so much to do.

When we got near the docks, we noticed something was different. It was busy like usual, but there seemed to be a lot more people doing a lot of loud talking. "What's going on?" I asked Pa.

"Don't know. I do know yesterday was election day. Maybe it has something to do with that."

When we got closer, I heard somebody shouting, "We don't need no slave-lover in the White House!" Lots of folks cheered.

"Will," Pa was real serious. "I think Lincoln won the election."

"What's that gonna mean? I know Buchanan is president now, and that didn't seem to make people mad."

"I'm not sure what it will mean, but it could be trouble. I've heard people talking about secession."

"What's that?"

"South Carolina would quit being in the United States and be its own country. We got the Palmetto Regiment to protect it, ships to keep the harbor safe. Citadel cadets can get real experience protecting the city. Maybe it wouldn't be all bad. Then all of this hullaballoo will be done." Pa sounded pretty sure.

I'd never heard of anybody quit being part of a country before. I wondered if the rest of the country would think it was a good idea.

While we were waiting our turn to sell the cotton, I listened to what the men were saying. Some of them were talking about secession, like Pa said. Some were calling Lincoln a baboon that should go back to the zoo. Some were saying we needed another election to get a different president. All those ideas were getting mixed up in my head. From what I had learned from the book about George Washington, it seemed like being president was a hard job even when everybody wanted you to be president. I couldn't image how hard it would be when so many people hated you.

After we finished at the dock, we made our way to the market. We got Sarah her candy and tried to do some other shopping, but there were so many people milling around, it was hard to move and we decided to put it off for a day when things settled down.

When we got to the Hawkins' place, I saw Terrance in the courtyard and called to him. "Hey, Terrance, what do you think about the election?"

"Don't know nothin' about no election, Mr. Will. What I do know is, it won't make no difference to me no matter what." He turned and went back to the garden.

Aunt Fran was in the kitchen as usual. She seemed in a state. "John, Will." She nodded at us. "Wait in the library. I'll send Sarah."

"I thought she'd be in the park with Miss Annie."

"After the election, Annie feels safer in the house and remember she does have to study her lessons, same as you do. I can't talk now." Aunt Fran left the room with a tray.

We went through the entryway into a room that was books from floor to ceiling on all four walls. I didn't know how anybody could read all those, but I sure wanted to try. In the middle of the room was a beautiful, huge globe. It had all the countries in the world painted on it.

"See, Pa. See all these places to go and learn about?" I stood over it afraid to touch it, when the door opened.

"Hello, McShane." It was Mr. Hawkins. "Fran told me you were here waiting for Sarah, so I thought I'd come down to talk to you."

Pa stood tall and looked Mr. Hawkins in the eye. "Good to see you again, sir. I hope you and Mrs. Hawkins are well." That all sounded real formal for Pa.

"Yes, thank you. Actually, she and I have been talking about you. Well, actually, we've been talking about Sarah."

I saw Pa take a deep breath. "Sir, I'm sorry if she's been any trouble. I know Fran works for you and shouldn't be spending time away. And Will and I truly are thankful for the time she's been allowed to stay. If it is too hard for Fran or causing you trouble, we'll make other arrangements if you just give me a little time."

"No, no, McShane, on the contrary. Sarah is a delightful child, and we've come to love her. Feel like she is one of our own. That's what I'd like to talk to you about. I know about Mrs. McShane, and I'm sorry for your loss. Sarah has been living here since she was an infant. This is her home."

"What are you saying?" Pa's voice was some louder now.

"I want you to think about something. We have come to love Sarah. I think she feels the same about us. Mrs. Hawkins thinks, or rather we think, it would be best for Sarah if this was truly her home. Having a youngster in the house again has been wonderful for us. What I'm getting at is that we would like to adopt Sarah."

Pa tried to interrupt, but Mr. Hawkins went on. "Please, don't answer now. Think about it as long as you'd like. Keep in mind, however, the opportunities she would have. The best care, tutors, and a chance at a significant social life. She would travel and meet important people. I'm sure you love her, but could you give her that? Please don't answer now."

He finished as the door opened and a servant brought Sarah into the room. She looked from Mr. Hawkins to Pa like she didn't know who to go to. I dropped to my knees and said, "Sarah, come give me a hug." She ran to me and started digging in my pockets until she found the peppermint. She was happy, and Mr. Hawkins and I smiled. Pa wasn't smiling. "Will," said Mr. Hawkins, changing the subject, "I saw you were interested in the globe."

"Yes, sir. I didn't touch it, sir."

"It's OK You can certainly touch it. I also have several books with maps in them. If you would like, you could borrow one or two of them. Just let Fran know which ones."

"Thank you, sir."

"Think about it, McShane. You and Will would always be welcome here, as you are now." He left Pa and me to stare at each other, trying to think through all he said, when Sarah started to squeal and climb on my shoulders.

We spent the rest of the afternoon at the park. Neither of us had any more thoughts about the election.

We were quiet for a while on the way home when I said, "Well, Pa, I was surprised you didn't tell Mr. Hawkins right off that you weren't goin' to give Sarah away."

It took Pa a minute to answer. "It's something to be thinkin' about. Too important not to give it some time."

"What are you sayin'? You're really thinkin' about givin' my sister to the Hawkins?"

"It ain't *givin'* her, Will. It's letting them adopt her. You heard Mr. Hawkins. Tutors, travel, important people. I could never give her that."

I usually let Pa have the last word, but not now. "Tutors? Important people? What about family? What about Ma? You think Ma would give her away for tutors? Why don't you just get married again so we can be a real family together? I love Ma, but she's gone, and we can't keep living like she'll come back and things will all be the same again." I had never talked to Pa like that and knew he'd probably wallop me for it, but I didn't care. He could do nothing that would hurt me more than giving up Sarah. I didn't wait to hear more. I ran. I didn't want to be near him.

I ran 'til I got almost home when Spike met me. "Come on, boy. Let's go down to the river." It was always a good place for me to think.

It was a long time before Pa came and sat down next to me. "I know what you're saying, son. But think it through. The Hawkins' place is the only home Sarah knows. She would have a lot more opportunities in the city than out there. We could still go visit her whenever we wanted. It wouldn't be no different than it is now." I stared at the river flowing by, wishing I could float away with it.

Pa kept talking. "I loved your mother more than you can imagine. I can't ever think about replacing her. So I ain't thought about gettin' married again."

There might be a fist coming upside my head, but I didn't care. "I never said replace Ma. She's my mother and Sarah's! It ain't goin' be the same. Never! Why can't we do it different? You talk about Sarah not knowing a home here. Why not? Why can't she be here? Do you think that's what Ma would do? We could make it work out. Pa, you talk about all those fancy opportunities! Why don't you give me away, too?" I got up and stomped back to the house.

I got into bed and turned my face to the wall. I didn't want to see or hear him no more today!

The next morning, I got up, did my chores, ate a big breakfast, and went to school without saying a word. Jimmy caught up to me right after I passed the fork in the road. "Hey, Will. What do you think about Lincoln getting elected? Ma's glad about it, but Grampa is mad as a wet hen."

"Ain't given it much thought, Jimmy. Had other things on my mind."

"You do look pretty serious, Will. Is there a problem?"

"Don't know if I should be talking about this, so don't say nothing. But Mr. Hawkins wants to adopt Sarah, and Pa is actually considering it."

"Wow. What do you think he'll do?"

"Don't know. He says she'll have lots more opportunities, but I think a family is more important." The rest of the walk to school was quiet.

We spent less time on numbers and reading than Mrs. Wilson talked about the new president. She asked Jimmy and me what we thought it would mean. We weren't sure, but we both thought it could cause trouble. I'd already heard that in town.

The next week was real quiet at home. I spent as much time as I could fishing and reading. Pa would ask about school, but my answers were short. I wanted to know what he was thinking, but I was afraid to ask.

CHAPTER 7

• • •

ONE DAY WHEN I CAME home from school, I saw something new in the cabin. It was a small bed.

"What's that for?"

"Well, if Sarah is going to get used to living here, she has to have a bed."

"Really, Pa? When is she coming to live here?" I felt like the whole world lifted off my shoulders.

"Slow down. It'll be a while longer, but I thought we could have her come for a few days sometimes to get used to the place, and it would give us time to learn how to take care of a little girl. How about if we go into town tomorrow after school? I can talk to Fran and tell Mr. Hawkins my decision."

"Yes, sir!" I did something I ain't done in a long time. I gave my pa a hug.

• • •

Pa was outside talking to Mr. Wilson the next day after school. On our way to town, he said, "Things will be a lot different with a little girl around. You won't be going fishing and hunting as much. There might be times you can't go to school or read because you'll be watching Sarah."

"Yes, sir. I think I'll teach her how to fish, and I can read to her." Then I chuckled. "Think she'll figure out I don't always have peppermint in my pocket?"

When we got to the Hawkins', Sarah was playing hide and seek in the courtyard with Terrance while Miss Annie and the lieutenant watched them.

Lt. Davis stood up when he saw us. "Will. Good to see you again. Sir." He nodded, looking at Pa.

"Jeff, this is Mr. McShane, Sarah and Will's father."

"I thought as much, Annie. It's a pleasure to meet you."

Pa greeted them and told me to stay outside and play while he went in to talk to Aunt Fran and Mr. Hawkins.

"Lieutenant," I asked, "I'm wondering what the soldiers think about Lincoln getting elected. Seems like everybody in town is in a state over it."

"It seems that way, Will. As far as the men at Fort Moultrie are concerned, I don't know that they think much about it. Since our regiment is mostly from up north, a lot of them agree with Lincoln. But even if they don't agree, we are all US soldiers, and whoever is the president is our commander, and we follow his orders."

"Do you think there will be trouble?"

"I hope not. General Gardner has just been replaced with Major Anderson as our commander here. He is a Southerner, and he has been to Charleston before. He knows some of the politicians from here. Hopefully, that will help to keep things quiet."

I was still curious. "What if South Carolina secedes, like I've heard talk about? Who would those soldiers listen to then?"

"That's a good question. I hope we don't have to find out. But if they are US soldiers, I guess it would be the president of the United States."

"I don't get why it's all so mixed up! Seems to me everybody could work on getting it figured out without getting so mad."

"I like the way you think, Will. Maybe someday you'll be president."

I didn't know what to say. I thought about George Washington and then Mr. Lincoln. At school, Mrs. Wilson told us his parents had been farmers like mine. His ma died, like mine. He didn't go to regular school, either. Maybe I *could* be president. I guessed it was best not to tell Pa that just now, though.

I played with Sarah and Terrance for a while 'til Pa came out. He was carrying a book.

"Will. I've talked to Fran. She was not real happy about it, but she'll help us. We'll come fetch Sarah on Saturday after we've been to the market to get our supplies. Fran will have some of Sarah's things ready so we can take her home for a few days. I talked to Mr. Hawkins, too. He understood and hoped it will all work out for us. He told me that Sarah would always have a home here. Oh, I almost forgot. He gave me this for you. Said you could keep it for a while."

"This is really something!" It was a huge book of maps that had the word "atlas" on the front. "Do you think I could take it to school if I'm real careful and don't let nobody touch it?"

"I expect you can."

We left them in the courtyard and headed home after telling Sarah she was coming to our house to visit in a few days. "Can we play hide and seek? Can we have peppermint?" she asked.

"We are going to do that and a lot more," said Pa. This was one of the few times Pa didn't look sad when we left.

On the way home, Pa said, "Will, I never thanked you."

"For what, Pa?"

"For reminding me that we are a family, even though Ma ain't here. For reminding me that we have to go on and have the best life we can. Together. Guess I had still been feeling sorry for myself. Now we have a big job ahead of us. It will be to move Sarah here, slow, so she doesn't get scared."

"She ain't scared of us, Pa."

"I know, but she don't understand it all yet. She could get scared about not seeing Fran or the Hawkins or the place she knows as her home. Think of her like a calf being weaned. There's no hurry as long as we keep working on it."

On Saturday, we took the wagon to town to get the supplies we hadn't gotten before. It was a lot quieter than it had been the last time we were here.

Pa stopped to talk to some of the other farmers. They talked about cotton prices and the weather. Then somebody asked Pa if he had heard that the secession talk was getting louder, and what did Pa think about secession? "Well, I think I'll leave that to the politicians and keep an eye on my crops," he answered. "I don't think they care what I think. I just want to be left to take care of my home and family."

They all nodded and agreed, but one farmer said, "Wish it could be that easy, John. This could cause trouble, as far as cotton prices go."

"Don't think so," said somebody else. "I hear that it could be a good thing. England would buy all the cotton we can raise, and nobody in Washington could say nothing about it. Besides, we don't need lots of black folks running around the country, looking to take our land away." The men nodded again.

When Pa and me left, I told him I thought he made sense, but so did the others. "I don't know what to think no more."

"It ain't an easy one to sort out, son. There's Sarah."

She was at the park, dressed in what looked like her Sunday best, sitting next to Miss Annie. "Sarah," I called. "Do you want to play hide and seek?"

"No, Willie. I'm all dressed up and acting like a lady." We all smiled. "Aunt Fran says I'm coming to visit you, and so I should behave."

"Well, you are coming to visit. But you don't have to behave too much."

She jumped up and was at my pocket, looking for the candy. Pa went in to get her things.

"Looks like you been teaching Sarah to be a lady." I looked at Miss Annie.

"Will, she is such a wonderful child. I'll miss her."

"She'll be back in a couple of days. Did Aunt Fran tell you we're planning on doing this a little at a time?"

"Yes, and maybe it's for the best. People in town seem to be getting more riled up. There's more secession talk, and I do worry about Jeff. I don't want the people here to hate the soldiers because they have been assigned here."

"I can't figure what there is to worry about. The lieutenant has the whole army behind him."

"I suppose you're right, Will. I hope so."

Sarah enjoyed the ride back to the cabin. She chattered and asked all sorts of questions about things she hadn't seen before. When we got back, Pa and I unloaded the wagon while she looked around. Then Pa started to get supper ready. "Where are the servants?" asked Sarah.

"We don't have servants," Pa answered. Sarah looked like she didn't understand. Pa was right. This would take a lot of getting used to for all of us.

We had decided to spend our first time with her just walking her around the farm, showing her the river, and watching the animals. She had fun helping to feed the chickens and liked the fresh milk.

Two days went by pretty fast, and Pa said he would take her back the next morning. He should be home by the time I got back from school.

In the morning, I hugged Sarah good-bye and told her we would play again real soon and I would teach her how to fish. I decided to take the book of maps to school.

All of the Wilsons were pretty surprised that there were so many different countries. I explained the little that I had heard about the people in each country living different than us. Jimmy showed us where he had lived, and Mrs. Wilson pointed out the places she had been. I decided then that there was more to learn than I had thought.

• • •

Pa and I spent the rest of the week catching up on the things we hadn't done while Sarah had been there. I was able to read a lot and was just about finished with the book on George Washington. I was hoping that the next time we went to the Hawkins', I would be able to borrow another book. Maybe Mr. Hawkins had one about Thomas Jefferson.

We had planned to go back for Sarah in a week or so, but the weather was bad. There was so much rain and the tides were so high that Pa was afraid the wagon would get stuck, so we would have to wait. When things finally dried out enough, it was getting colder, so we put some blankets in the wagon when we went into town.

The first stop was the market. Pa had brought some extra eggs and some nails he wouldn't need. While he was trying to sell our extra, I asked him if I could go to the docks to see if there were some sailors I could talk to. "You go on," he said. "Meet me at the Hawkins' in a while. Remember, we got to leave early, or the sun will be down before we get back."

I hurried to the docks and was surprised at what I saw. I figured by this time of the year, things would be slowing down, but they were busier than usual. "What's goin' on?" I asked a dock hand.

"Oh, you mean 'cause we have the docks so full? I think a lot of folks are trying to stock up on some goods and ship out everything that they can. Lots of rumors about secession and the army shutting down the port."

"How could the army shut down the port?"

"Don't know. Like I said, lots of rumors. Not sure what to believe except that lots of folks ain't happy with the way things are right now."

I wasn't sure why there were rumors going around. Didn't seem to me like anything had changed. I wandered around to see if there was a sailor that had time to talk about places he'd been, but everybody was real busy loading and unloading so I went on to the Hawkins'.

I found Aunt Fran in the kitchen, working on her books and lists. She asked me how I was and how I was liking school. "I like it just fine. Wish I had more time and we had more books, but it's sure better than not going. Do you think that Mr. Hawkins might have a book about Thomas Jefferson that I could borrow? I read the one Ma had about George Washington. I brought the map book back. Pa has it in the wagon. He should be along anytime."

"Your mother would be proud of you. I know there are a lot of books, but I don't know what they are all about. Joseph would know. Let's go find him and ask." Joseph was the black butler. We found him in the dining room, giving the house servants instructions on polishing the silver and arranging the crystal glasses.

"Joseph, would you be able to take a few minutes and help Will try to find a book in Mr. Hawkins' library? I know he wouldn't mind. We have talked about Will being able to borrow a book from time to time."

"Yes, ma'am. I believe they can finish without me." He nodded at the maids. "Follow me, Mr. Will."

He led me to the library, where I said, "Please, just call me Will. Are there any books about Thomas Jefferson?"

"I don't know how to read very much, I'm sorry to say. But I do know Mr. Hawkins has his books all in order so he can find what he wants. All the books about people are over here on this wall, mostly on the bottom six shelves. I know because we had them out to dust last week."

I looked around at what must have been hundreds or thousands of books. "You dusted all of these?"

"Yes, Mr. Will. We have to take them out and take care that bugs don't get into them and start chewing on the pages." I gave up on him leaving off the mister from my name. He went on, "I don't know 'zactly where to look, but if you want to see if you can find one, maybe I can help."

Just then, there was the sound of breaking glass and a high-pitched scream. Joseph ran toward the door. "You look, Mr. Will. I'll come back." He ran out of the room.

I did look. I started at the bottom and looked at every book on each shelf. I didn't know how long this could take. Then the door opened. Without turning around I said, "Joseph, I don't think there is any way I'll find what I want."

"What do you want, Will?" It wasn't Joseph. I jumped up and turned around to see Mr. Hawkins smiling down at me.

"Sir, Aunt Fran and Joseph said I could look for a book about Thomas Jefferson. I didn't mean no harm."

"Of course there's no harm. I'm happy to let you use the books. That is what they are for. Let's see. Jefferson is here, with all the other biographies of presidents." He put his hand on a shelf that had three books about the author of the Declaration of Independence. He took them down and gave them to me. "Take a look through them and see which one you would like." I picked out the thinnest one. It would still take me a long time to read, so I was hoping to get the most information the fastest from that one. "When you finish that one, tell me what you think about it. How did you like the atlas?"

"Pa's bringing that back shortly. I took it to school," I confessed. "But I didn't let nobody touch it. We looked at all the places in the world, and Mrs. Wilson told us a little about some of them that she knew about. There sure are lots of countries."

"There are. It's fine that you took it to school. Do you know there may be one more country that's not in the atlas? There's so much talk about secession that maybe South Carolina will be a separate country. Did you know that Governor Gist has called for a secession convention so people can vote whether to secede or not? It will be coming up the week before Christmas. That may be a good gift for all of us."

"I been hearing about that. Can't figure out what it all would mean, though."

Mr. Hawkins went on, "It would mean that we could all keep our servants, and plantations could keep their slaves to grow the cotton that helps to make Charleston a rich city."

"So secession would be a good thing?"

"I believe it would. We could create our own government and laws and live the life that suits us."

Just then, I heard Pa calling at the library door. "Mr. Hawkins. Will, are you ready to go? Sarah is all set to spend a few more days with us." He handed the atlas to Mr. Hawkins. "I can't thank you enough for all you are doing."

"It's my pleasure, McShane. It seems like everybody is happy this way. Your boy has interest in a lot of things. I admire the way you are raising him. Good day." He walked out before Pa could answer.

CHAPTER 8

• • •

"Gee, Pa. It sure is interesting talking to Mr. Hawkins. He said the governor is going to have a secession convention. Who's gonna vote on it?" We were on our way home with Sarah bundled in a blanket, sitting on my lap. The weather had gotten colder, and it was easy to tell winter was close.

"I heard tell that there are delegates going to Columbia to vote. It's coming up real soon. I'm pretty sure they'll vote for it. Don't know if it's a good thing or a bad thing."

"Mr. Hawkins thinks it's a good thing. Says everybody here can make their own laws and keep their slaves, 'cause that's what works best here."

"Maybe he's right."

"Willie, not so tight!" I guess I had been holding on to Sarah a little more than I needed to.

"Sorry. Tomorrow we'll go fishing, and I'll show you my favorite spot to catch big fish. Would you like that?"

"Goody!"

"Pa, I'm planning to stay home from school while Sarah is with us. Then I can help, and we can get chores and things done."

"That's a good idea, Will. We can see about it the day after. We all have to start getting used to living together and still doing the things that need to get done. Way I see it, one of the things you need to get done is goin' to school. I said that your ma would have been proud of you, but I want you to know that I'm proud of you, too."

"Thanks, Pa." It wasn't like Pa to talk like that. It made me feel good.

Later on, when Pa was getting Sarah ready for bed, I was looking at the book about Thomas Jefferson. I found the Declaration of Independence that he wrote. I had trouble with some of the words and what they meant, but I was working through them. This made me even more mixed up.

"Pa, you ever hear the Declaration of Independence read? Listen and maybe you can help me figure it out. 'When in the course of human events, it becomes necessary for one people to dissolve the political bands which have connected them with another...' and then some stuff I don't get. But at the end it says 'that they should declare the causes which impel them to the separation.' Dissolve means to make it go away, right? And political bands, is that like government? Does it mean that the government should go away?"

"That's what it seems like to me, Will. I know there was a war with England so the colonies could be free from them. I guess they didn't like what England was doing anymore."

"Ain't that like what the secession convention would be about? If South Carolina doesn't like what the government is doing it can break away, just like what Jefferson said?"

Pa shrugged, and I looked over more of the Declaration. There was lots I didn't get, but I got to thinking. "We went to war with England. But I thought England is our friend now and buys a lot of our cotton. If we're friends now, how come we went to war? Why didn't we just figure it out with England?"

"Son, I can't answer that. I guess it's like having an argument with a friend and then getting along again."

"I got lots of questions to ask Mrs. Wilson. I guess secession must be right if Jefferson said so, and he was a president." I gave Sarah a hug and tucked her into bed. I went back to the book to read about how Jefferson got to be president.

We were busy the next day with fishing and playing. Sarah seemed to be happy here. She liked the animals and liked to run outside and play with Spike.

When I went back to school, I asked about the things Pa and I had talked about. Mrs. Wilson said she didn't know the answer about being bad or good but thought we would know in a few days after the convention.

• • •

We took Sarah back to the Hawkins' the day before the convention was supposed to happen in Columbia. We saw Miss Annie in the courtyard. She looked fretful.

"Is there something wrong, Miss Annie?" Pa asked.

"Oh, Mr. McShane. You startled me. I'm very worried about this secession talk. Well, it's more than talk now. It was supposed to happen in Columbia tomorrow, but it's being moved to Charleston because of a smallpox outbreak there. The delegates want to stay away from that disease. I'm worried about what will happen to Jeff and the rest of the garrison at Fort Moultrie. They are US Army troops. If South Carolina secedes, what will they do? Go back to New York? Stay at the fort? Give up the fort? Will the South Carolina regiment attack them? Jeff says that Major Anderson doesn't plan to change anything until it happens and he gets orders from Washington."

"Miss Annie," said Pa, "why not wait and see before you fret so. Maybe it will all get worked out."

"I do try to be calm about it, Mr. McShane, but I just can't stop worrying." She took a deep breath and tried to smile. "Now, Sarah, come give me a hug. I missed you." Sarah seemed happy here, too. Maybe this going back and forth could work for a long time.

Pa went in to let Aunt Fran know we were back with Sarah and came out with a broken chair. "Seems that one of the servants accidentally broke this, and Fran would like me to fix it before Mr. Hawkins finds out. She said the girl is trying real hard but has had a string of bad luck. Fran doesn't want her to get into trouble."

Miss Annie smiled. "I think I know who she is talking about. If it is Marion, she dropped a whole tray of crystal a while ago, and Mrs. Hawkins had a fit. She's a sweet girl but seems a bit clumsy."

On the way home Pa seemed to be thinking out loud. "I hope Miss Annie's brother is safe. It sure all seems like a hornets' nest."

"What could happen, Pa?"

"Maybe nothing. Maybe some hothead cadets from the Citadel will think it's a good idea to take some potshots at the US Army. We'll have to wait and see."

• • •

A few days later, we heard about the convention when Jimmy came running into school, waving a newspaper. "Look at this!" We mostly didn't get a chance to see newspapers, so we were happy to look at it.

I read the headline that was in big black letters. "'The Union is Dissolved!'" Dissolved. That was the same word Jefferson used. It worked then. Maybe it would work now, but without a war.

Jimmy told us, "Grampa was so excited about it, he bought a paper to show Ma. She's not happy at all but doesn't say much. She doesn't want to make him mad, and that would upset Pa. He isn't feeling good."

"Well," said Mrs. Wilson as she put her arm around Jimmy's shoulders. "It looks as if your father will have to get better in a different country than he was in yesterday." Jimmy nodded.

"I don't get it. Mr. Lincoln isn't even president yet. Why didn't they just wait to see if they could work things out?"

"I don't know, William. Maybe they wanted to send him a message that they meant what they said." I'd have to think on that.

I thought about it all the way home from school without figurin' it out. Pa had the chair fixed by the time I got there and asked if I wanted to go with him to take it back to Aunt Fran. "You bet I do. I want to know what's all going on."

We got into town to find the streets filled with lots of folks. Some were smiling, some shouting, some drunk, but mostly, they seemed like they were celebrating.

Aunt Fran seemed upset. "Everything is so topsy-turvey! People were out on the battery all night, shouting and carrying on. Could hardly sleep. Mr. Hawkins is pleased, Miss Annie is scared for her brother, and I don't know what to think. Are you going to take Sarah with you today?"

"Don't think so, Fran. How about we come back and pick her up right before Christmas? That way we can spend it together, like a family."

"That's fine with me. Do you want to see her now? I believe she is playing with Terrance."

"Let's just slip out without her seeing us today. It's getting late, and we have to be headed back before it gets dark. We'll be back in a couple of days. We'll be able to stop at the market and get the doll that I saw the other day."

"All right, John. Thank you for fixing the chair. I'll tell Marion to be more careful."

I was wandering around the market two days later while Pa went to find the doll he wanted to get for Sarah. When I looked back, I saw him talking to a group of men and they all seemed excited. Maybe it was because of talk I heard about other states seceding, too. I heard some folks talking about Alabama and Mississippi. Somebody said they thought Georgia would join in, and all those states could make up a separate country. I wondered if that was what Thomas Jefferson had in mind back in 1776.

When Pa and I met up again, he had some packages under his arm. I asked him what he had in those.

"Will, you never ask about packages two days before Christmas." Even with all the hullaballoo going on, Pa seemed happier, and he smiled more.

While we were waiting in the kitchen for Aunt Fran to fetch Sarah, Mr. Hawkins came in. He had a package, too. "Will, this is for you. Merry Christmas."

"Thank you, sir. I don't have a present for you."

"That's quite all right. I have to admit, I'm doing this as much for myself as for you." I didn't know what he meant, but he went on, "Go on, open it."

When I took the paper off, I almost dropped the present. It was the atlas he had let me borrow. "Mr. Hawkins, I couldn't take your book!"

"I want you to have it, Will. I want you to take it to school, and you can let the others touch it if you'd like. I said I was doing this for myself, too. I am enjoying watching you learn. Your curiosity is going to take you a long way. Maybe I can help a little."

"Thank you, sir. I'll take good care of it, and if you ever decide you want it back, I'll understand."

"I won't want it back. I want you to look at those places and learn about them. Maybe someday you can go to some of them. Now, I hear Sarah coming. She may want to bring her new tea set along. That was our gift to her. I hope all of the McShanes have a very merry Christmas!"

Pa swallowed hard. "Thank you, sir. This is going to be a special day for us."

• • •

We got Sarah home with her new tea set. It was hard not to tell her that she would have a new doll to have tea parties with.

Pa had cut down a small fir for our Christmas tree. We didn't have no fancy ornaments, but we cut holly branches off of the bushes behind the cabin, and we had some paper that we each drew a picture on and hung on the tree. We even had a small candle fixed on the top. It was our first Christmas tree and our first Christmas all together.

Sarah was surprised at the size of our tree, because the Hawkins' tree had taken up a good part of the parlor. "Little," she kept saying.

"It is little, but it is ours. And maybe Santa will come tonight with a present for you," I replied.

"Who's Santa?"

I realized that since the Hawkins' children were grown, they probably didn't talk about Santa anymore. "He's the man that comes at Christmas to leave good little girls and boys presents."

"Where does he come from?"

I looked at Pa. I wasn't sure what to say when he said, "From very far away. Have you been a good girl?"

She nodded 'til I thought she'd shake off her hair. Pa and I laughed. This *would* be a special day.

• • •

The next morning when we woke up, there were two packages under the tree. One had Sarah's name on it, and one had mine. Of course, there was a squeal of excitement when she opened her new doll. It had a fancy dress, yellow hair, and even little shoes. She was delighted and sat down immediately with her doll and a teacup.

I looked at the other package and then at Pa. "Looks like Santa brought you a present too, Will. I suppose that means you were a good boy." He had a big smile on his face.

"Willie is good. Come play."

"In a minute, Sarah." I unwrapped my package and saw a book called *Places around the World*. It wasn't very big, but when I opened it, I saw that it was about some of the countries that I had seen in my new atlas. I couldn't think of anything to say. All I could do was hug Pa. "Thank you, Pa," I finally sputtered. "Now I can look at a place, see where it is, and learn something about it!"

"Not Pa! Santa!"

"Yes, Sarah, Santa. Now, we'll play with your doll, and then we will sit at the table and pretend we're at school, and I'll read to you about another country."

"Me and Dolly!"

"Yes, you and Dolly." It was a truly special day.

CHAPTER 9

• • •

I SPENT THE NEXT TWO days drinking water out of little teacups and reading about different countries. The weather was different there, the houses were different, the clothes were different, the people did different things. I never knew there could be so many differences.

By the time we had to take Sarah back to Charleston, she was getting antsy. It was cold, and we couldn't spend too much time outside. Even tea parties were not as much fun anymore.

We bundled up, hitched Gray onto the wagon, and headed for town with Dolly on Sarah's lap. Since we had been going in the wagon so much because Sarah couldn't walk that far, the trip was pretty quick. We didn't figure it would take long, and Pa said that I could go to the dock for a while to talk to the sailors. He said he wanted to spend some time with Aunt Fran.

We never expected what we found when we got into town. We thought people were mad after the election, but this was lots worse. The battery was full of people. Rich people, poor people, slaves, Citadel cadets, South Carolina regiment soldiers milling around. Lots of them were yelling and some just staring out into the harbor.

We saw Terrance in the crowd, and I asked him what was going on. "Look there, Mr. Will." He pointed out toward the new fort in the harbor. "They's moved into the fort, and all these folks said they can't do that, but they did. You can see the flag flying from here."

Terrance wasn't making sense. "They moved into Fort Sumter? Who did?"

"Them Yankee soldiers. Miss Annie's brother. I even heard folks talkin' about war."

"Let's go find Fran. Maybe she can explain."

We went into the kitchen and found Aunt Fran with her arm around a crying Miss Annie. "What's happening?" asked Pa. He was getting upset because he didn't know what was going on, but it seemed pretty important.

"Oh, Mr. McShane!" wailed Annie.

Aunt Fran started to explain that the flag of the United States was flying over Fort Sumter.

"But it belongs to the US Army," said Pa.

"I know that, but it seems lots of folks believed that since South Carolina seceded, the fort should belong to South Carolina and that the US Army should leave it. We are not part of the United States any more. Lots of people are saying this is an act of war and the militia can defend us from invaders."

"They ain't invaders," I said. "They been here a long time."

"That's not how most people see it, Will." There was another sob.

"Miss Annie is very upset about her brother. She has no idea what has happened to him or what will happen to her."

Just then there was a knock at the door. A man in tattered clothes stood there with a piece of paper in his hand. Aunt Fran sounded angry as she told him, "Not now! I can't get you anything to eat. Can't you see there is a problem here? Go away!"

"Ma'am," the man stuttered. "I ain't come for nothing to eat. I was working on the fort when boats came last night with soldiers and told us that we could stay if we wanted to work and were on the side of Lincoln and the US Army. I can't do that. My family's here. Don't know what would happen to 'em iffin I didn't come back."

"Did you come here to tell us you are loyal? I don't care!" She was really mad now.

"No, ma'am. I came because the lieutenant asked me to deliver this to somebody named Annie Davis."

Miss Annie jumped up and grabbed the paper out of the man's hand. Aunt Fran looked a little sheepish and walked over to a jar on the shelf. She took out a coin and gave it to the man before she closed the door, almost in his face.

"This is from Jeff. It must mean he is all right." She opened the letter and read,

Dearest Annie,

I am writing this to tell you that I am well, as are all of the men in the regiment. Last night, Major Anderson decided that we must move out of Fort Moultrie while he awaits orders from Washington. He felt the safest place for us was here at Fort Sumter because we could not defend ourselves at Moultrie. He gave us only ten minutes to gather our belongings and get into the boats. We were able to sneak past the ships guarding the harbor and now feel quite safe here. I expect President Buchanan will send orders for us to evacuate the fort soon. When those orders come, you will be going back with me, so be aware that you may have to be ready to leave on short notice. Don't worry about me. We are in good spirits and have enough supplies to keep us for a while. We will likely be able to continue to get supplies from town. I will try to get into the city to make arrangements and to see you. Continue with your studies.
Your loving brother,
Jefferson

Miss Annie let out a long sigh. "That is such a relief. I hope they get orders soon. I am so afraid for him and beginning to feel uncomfortable myself."

Sarah hugged her leg. "Don't be sad."

"No, Sarah. I won't be sad now."

• • •

On the way home I told Pa that none of the goings-on made sense to me. I couldn't figure why the Yankees couldn't go home, and I couldn't figure why they needed to. They weren't attacking Charleston. From what I heard, there weren't enough of them to do much of anything.

"I don't understand either, Will. I heard some people on the battery calling it an act of war. I don't know why they won't be patient until President Buchanan orders them to give up the fort. I'm sure he'll do that, and all the ruckus will be done with."

"An act of war? You don't think there'll be a war, do you, Pa?"

"I doubt it. It sounds like a lot of hothead talk. Won't amount to much as long as nobody starts shootin'."

• • •

I found out two days later that Pa might be wrong about the war talk. At school, Mrs. Wilson told us she heard that the US arsenal at Castle Pinckney surrendered and the secessionist flag was flying over that fort in the harbor.

"Who did that, and why? Does it belong to South Carolina?" I asked.

"The South Carolina regiment did it because they don't want the Yankees to have any more weapons than they have, William. I believe the regiment thinks they do own it now that South Carolina is a separate country."

On the way home from school, I asked Jimmy what he thought about all of the goin's-on.

"Haven't been paying much attention, Will. Pa's been real sick, so I've been trying to help out more. We're all real worried about him."

The weather had been cold and rainy, so I could understand that somebody that had trouble breathing could be worse. "Sorry to hear that. Bet he'll be better when the weather warms up in a while."

"Yeah. Bet you're right."

• • •

When we went to get Sarah again, we saw all kinds of boats in the harbor. They weren't all the kind that brought things in and out at the dock. They were all sizes and seemed to be floating around in circles. I asked Pa if I could go down to the dock to see what was happening. He told me to go ahead, because he had to talk to Aunt Fran anyway, and he would be a while.

When I asked one of the sailors, he said, "They're patrolling the harbor. Don't want those Yankees playing any more tricks like the last time."

"What kind of tricks do they think they'll play?"

"Maybe getting supplies and reinforcements. Can't trust them folks in Washington now any more than we can trust Lincoln and his Black Republicans."

That was the first time I heard of Black Republicans. I could pretty well guess it meant somethin' about the folks that were against slavery. "What are they doing over there?" I asked him, pointing up the Cooper River. "If they're building a ship, it don't look much like it'll go far."

"Ain't no ship. They're building a floating battery so's they can get cannons close enough to Sumter if they need 'em. Guess they figure the other forts ain't enough, so they're doing that, and they got cadets at Morris Island digging some earthworks. Looks like they'll have the fort surrounded. Now get out of my way, boy. I gotta get these supplies loaded to take out to the island with the tide at first light."

I tried to puzzle all of this out. There were US soldiers in a fort that was part of the United States that was in Charleston Harbor—that was a part of the United States until a few weeks ago. Those soldiers had been sent here to protect the harbor, but now the South Carolina Regiment was fixin' to shoot at 'em. I still had trouble figuring how this was about slavery. Soldiers had been around here as long as I could remember. I seen them at the market and in the city now and again. There were slaves here for a long time too. Why couldn't it still be that way? It didn't make sense. I thought about it all the way to the Hawkins' house but still couldn't sort through it.

In the Hawkins' courtyard I heard Mr. Hawkins and another man talking. The other man said, "But you have a lot of influence at the dock. Why would it be so hard for you to find some way to get this message to Morris Island and my son? His mother is sick. I'm afraid she might be dying, and he's out there playing soldier. He needs to be here!"

"Calm down, Burke. I know you're upset. My influence is with shippers, not the dockhands that are moving supplies around the harbor and I certainly know of no one going out to Morris Island."

"I do, sir." I spoke up before I thought that maybe I should keep quiet. They both looked at me.

"Go on, Will. What do you know?"

"I know that there's a boat of supplies going over there when the tide goes out tomorrow. I just talked to one of the men that was loading the boat."

"Boy, take this and run ask him to deliver it to Cadet Charles Burke. Hurry."

"Tell my pa I'll be right back." I ran as fast as I could back to the dock and found the boat being loaded with food and tools. I also found the man I had talked to before who seemed to be the leader. "Mister," I panted. "Will you take this letter to Morris Island tomorrow with the supplies and give it to Cadet Burke? It's real important—about his ma!"

"Look, I ain't playing nursemaid to nobody. I got business to do. If you want it delivered, do it yourself. I'd let you go if you'll help finish getting this loaded before dark. There's been so much going on around here, we're short-handed. I can use some help but I ain't got money."

"I'd need to ask my pa."

"You do that. If you're back here right away, you can help. Tell him we leave at first light and should be back around dinnertime."

Off I went again. Wasn't runnin' as fast, but I thought it was important. I wanted to help Mr. Hawkins because he'd been doin' so much for us. I also knew that a mother being sick was about the worst thing that could happen. The cadet needed to know.

"Pa! Pa!" I could hardly breathe by the time I got back. After I explained what was happening and why I thought I should go, he didn't say anything for a minute. "Can I? Can I do it?"

"How would you get back here by first light?"

"The boy can stay here." Mr. Hawkins had just walked into the kitchen where Pa and Aunt Fran were sitting at the table. "McShane, this is important, and I admire your boy for making the offer. We'll take care of him tonight, and I'll have one of the servants bring him home tomorrow. It would be a great help to my friend."

Pa nodded, and I was just about off again when Aunt Fran said, "You be back as soon as you can, Will. I'll have supper for you."

"Thanks, Aunt Fran. Tell Sarah I'll see her tomorrow."

• • •

Those crates and barrels and bundles all must have weighed a hundred pounds each. I heaved and pushed and pulled as hard as I could for what seemed like hours. The sun was just about down when we finished.

"First thing tomorrow, boy. Hey, what's your name? You're a good worker for a scrawny kid, and I don't want to keep calling you 'boy.'"

"Will McShane, sir. First light."

I dragged all of my aching muscles back to the Hawkins' and the supper that Aunt Fran had promised me. Even though I hurt all over, it felt good to be able to help Mr. Burke and his son. Made me miss my ma some, too.

The supper that Aunt Fran made was lots better than what Pa and I usually have. I was glad I could stay awake for a second piece of chocolate cake. I wasn't awake much longer, though. She had made up a bed for me just outside the kitchen. She told me that there was always a lot of activity around the kitchen in the morning, so I would have no problem waking up. She would leave bread and jam on the table for me.

She was still talking when I fell asleep.

• • •

AUNT FRAN WAS RIGHT. THERE was lots of noise early. I jumped up, grabbed the letter and the bread she left me, and raced out the door into the day. As I was going through the city, it looked like it was waking up. I had never been here this early. Wagons were taking crops to market, lamps were being lit in the houses, and servants and workers were moving around to get their jobs started. It felt peaceful and comfortable. I hoped it never changed.

At the dock, I found the sailor checking the lashes on the supplies. "Don't want anything sliding off. Mornin', Will. See you made it. Tom's coming. He's going out with us. Mornin', Tom."

"G'day, Mr. Jake. Who's this?" Tom looked at me.

"This is Will. He'll be givin' us a hand, and he's got a special delivery to make. Let's move. Tide's goin' out. Need to get there and unloaded so's I can come back when the tide turns."

Mr. Jake untied the boat, shoved off, and hoisted the sail. There wasn't much wind at the dock, but it was the tide that carried us out into the harbor where the sails caught what little breeze there was. The sky overhead was just turning orange.

We were getting close to Morris Island when we saw some blue and red lights on one of the ships in the harbor. "What's that for, Mr. Jake?"

"That is one of the patrol boats. They call her *Clinch*, and I think she might be signaling that other ship at the mouth of the harbor."

Just then, the *Clinch* turned and headed back toward the harbor. We saw bright flashes of light above her bow and then heard the booms. "What's going on, Mr. Jake?"

"Maybe it's the supply ship I been hearin' about. Look!" He pointed at the unknown ship farther out in the ocean. "Looks like a big American flag! I don't like this. Let's get around the island and anchored as quick as we can. I want to get these powder kegs off my boat! Hoist that other sail!"

When we rounded the end of Morris Island to find an out-of-the-way place to anchor, we passed a high mound of sand with a flag flying on it. The flag was red with a palmetto tree on it. I'd seen others like that and knew it was the secessionist flag. The cadets were running around, and somebody was screaming, "Prepare for action!"

We were trying to get the boat behind the backside of that mound of sand. There were cannons set and pointing toward the harbor. The cadets scattered but seemed to know where they were runnin' to. "Boy, tie down that sail! Tom, drop the anchor! Stay low! I think we'll have to sit this out here!"

I turned to see groups of cadets at the cannons and heard somebody yell, "Number one, fire!"

I'd never been that close to a cannon when it was fired. I thought for sure the noise would knock me down.

"Number two, fire!" I could only imagine how loud it would be if they shot them all at the same time.

"Number three, fire!" Between shots there was scurrying around to get the next round ready. All the shots looked like they missed. By the time they started the next round, the shooting didn't seem so loud. Maybe I couldn't hear nothing at all no more.

Well, I did hear something—loud cheering. One of the balls hit the ship, but before they could get off another shot, the ship had turned away. It wasn't over, though.   As the ship was getting farther from Morris Island it was getting closer to Sullivan's Island, and there were shots coming from Fort Moultrie. That ship headed out to sea and was not likely comin' back.

Morris Island erupted in cheers. "We beat 'em!"

"We showed those damn Yankees!"

"Bet they're sorry they ever tried this!"

Mr. Jake shook me out of my shock by yelling, "Let's get this stuff off my boat and get out of here!" He, Tom, and I started unloading while the celebrating settled down. It didn't take long until some of the cadets came to help. We were just about finished when I remembered the letter in my pocket.

"I've got to find Cadet Charles Burke!" I shouted as loud as I could over the dying cheers.

"That's me," said one of the men. "Who are you?"

"I brought a letter from your father." He looked at me suspicious-like, so I went on to explain how I had met his father at the Hawkins'. I decided not to tell him I knew what was in the letter. He'd find out soon enough.

We were starting to pull up anchor when he shouted to Mr. Jake to stop and asked us to wait just a few minutes while he talked to his commander and packed his knapsack. He was on the boat in no time and real quiet.

I wanted to ask him how it felt to fire a cannon, but I didn't figure it was a good time for that. Instead, I said, "I hope your ma will be better. My ma died. Sure hope yours doesn't."

He looked at me with a little smile, but he wiped away a tear on his cheek and looked down the rest of the way back to Charleston.

The city was buzzing when we got back. There were red secessionist flags flying all over. The battery was filling up with folks. They were standing around, some cheering and some looking out into the harbor, hoping to see more happening. But it was over, and I was relieved. If that was what war would sound like, I wanted to be as far away as I could.

• • •

It was a slow walk to the Hawkins'. I had to tell Aunt Fran I had delivered the letter and that I didn't want a servant to take me home. I needed to walk. I needed to think. I needed the quiet.

Miss Annie was in the kitchen with Aunt Fran. She was all upset about her brother. I told her, "Miss Annie, ain't nothin' to worry about. Wasn't no firing at the fort. It was at the ship bringing supplies. It turned around and left. Guess it's all over for now." I don't know why I said "for now." Everybody in the street seemed to think it was over and Sumter would be evacuated and the Yankees would be gone. I hoped they were right.

I felt some better by the time I got home. Sarah helped. "Take me fishing, Willie. Pa said we could. Want to go fishing now."

"In a minute." I laughed. Then I looked at Pa. "Lots happened since last night. I'll tell you about it after our fish dinner. Come on, Sarah." Sarah, Spike, and I headed to the river.

We brought back a string of fish, and Pa cooked up sweet potatoes that he makes special. We had to set the table for four, because Dolly was coming for dinner. Sarah always made us smile. We couldn't believe someone so small could fill our home the way that Sarah did. I was glad to be safe in a place I belonged.

After her big fishing trip and dinner, Sarah got sleepy fast. Pa got her ready for bed. "Read to me, Willie."

"OK. I'll read you the last pages about Thomas Jefferson. Then I can take Mr. Hawkins his book back and get another one. What do you think I should get a book about, Sarah?"

She thought for a minute. "A book about fairy princesses. Miss Annie reads me books about fairy princesses."

"OK, Sarah. I'll see if I can borrow one of those books about princesses."

As soon as she was asleep, I told Pa everything I had seen at Morris Island and everything I heard in town.

Pa nodded. "I was afraid of that. Fran told me the rumors about a supply ship coming with reinforcements."

"Why don't they just go home, Pa?"

"Don't know, son. I wish they would so things could go back to the way they were."

It took a long time for me to get to sleep. I kept hearing the guns go off. When I did sleep, I dreamed our cabin was exploding.

I was groggy in the morning, but I really wanted to go to school. There was a lot to tell everyone, and I was feeling proud that I had been there. It was late when I left home, so I missed catching Jimmy on the way.

"Good morning, William. I'm glad you could be here today," said Mrs. Wilson. "Since you've had to miss a few days, I'd like you to start by reciting the multiplication table for eights and nines."

"Yes, ma'am. But before I do, can I tell y'all what happened in Charleston yesterday?"

"If you think it was that important, go ahead."

I told the story like I told it to Pa the night before, only this time, I left out the part about being scared.

• • •

"You take Sarah back tomorrow, Will," Pa told me after she had been with us for almost a week. We all seemed to be settlin' into a pretty good routine when she was there. "I'm going to the Widow Caldwell's tomorrow. It's been a real long cold spell, and I know her boy's arm has healed pretty good, but they may need some help with more firewood."

"Sure, Pa." I was thinkin' maybe Pa would start courting the widow, but even if he didn't, I was hopin' for another sweet-potato pie.

Sarah chattered all the way back. When she wasn't talking to me, she was tellin' Dolly about fishin' and fairy princesses. That reminded me that I needed to ask Mr. Hawkins about a book for her.

At the Hawkins place, I left Sarah in the kitchen talking Aunt Fran's ears off and headed toward the library to return the Jefferson book. I hoped to find Mr. Hawkins but found Miss Annie and Lt. Davis instead. I overheard him tellin' Miss Annie that they were running low on supplies at the fort and he was hoping to arrange to buy some like they had done when they were at Fort Moultrie.

"I don't think buying the foodstuffs will be difficult. I think I will have more trouble finding a way to transport them out to the fort. Everybody at the dock seems to be busy with provisions and building a floating battery for the South Carolina regiment. I wish they would stop and think about it. We have eighty-five men at the fort, not counting the laborers. How could we ever attack Charleston?" He sighed deep.

"I think I can help." Again, I talked before I thought it through.

"Oh, Will." said Miss Annie. "I didn't know you were there."

"Sorry, ma'am. I shouldn't have interrupted, but I know a man with a boat. He may be able to help you."

"And who might that be?" asked the lieutenant.

"I call him Mr. Jake. I helped him take a load of supplies to Morris Island a time back. Maybe he would take your supplies, too. I could ask him."

"When could you do that?"

"Right away. I'd like to see Mr. Hawkins and ask him if he has a book about the Revolutionary War that I could borrow." I looked down at my feet and added, quiet-like, "and a book about fairy princesses."

The lieutenant looked surprised, but Miss Annie laughed. "I can help you with that," she said. Mr. Hawkins isn't here now, but I think Joseph can help you with the other one."

After I collected the books I wanted, Lt. Davis and I headed toward the wharf. We found Mr. Jake sitting on a crate, smoking his pipe. The lieutenant explained what he was interested in and what the pay would be. Mr. Jake sucked his pipe a couple times before he said, "I don't hold with no Yankees in the harbor, but business is business. I'll do it on one condition." He looked at me. "I'll only do it if Will is goin' to help me. Too few extra hands around here."

"Yes, sir. I'm sure my pa will let me."

"Pay you a dollar for the trip if you work like you did before."

"A dollar! I *know* Pa will let me."

"It's a good deal for everybody," said Lt. Davis. "I'm going now to get those provisions lined up. What do you say if I get them delivered here tomorrow and you bring them out the next day?"

"I'll shake on it, Lieutenant. Will, have I got your promise?"

"Yes, sir. I'll be here day after tomorrow."

• • •

"William, don't ever do that again!" Pa sure is mad when he calls me William. "Last time you did that, you were caught in shooting!"

"But, Pa, a dollar!"

"If you live through it! What if they start shootin' again?"

I hadn't thought of that. "Pa, I promised and Mr. Jake said he won't go without me."

Pa shook his head. "Boy, you caught me in a corner. You say you promised?"

"Yes, sir, and you always said to never break a promise."

"I know that. That's the only reason I'll let you go. But you will not do it again without talking to me first!"

"No, sir. Did the Caldwells need help?" I figured changin' the subject was a good idea.

"They did. The boy's arm ain't healed like it should be. It's sort of crooked and not very strong. Don't know what they'll do, but they'll need us to help out now and then until the little ones can do more. Almost forgot. Mary—I mean Mrs. Caldwell—sent fresh bread and blueberry preserves."

It wasn't the sweet-potato pie I had hoped for, but I knew I wouldn't be disappointed.

CHAPTER 11

• • •

I DECIDED TO GO TO school the next day to get caught up with numbers, and I wanted to show Mrs. Wilson the book about the Revolutionary War. She seemed to know something about everything. I was sure glad I could learn from her. On the way there, I saw my friend Jimmy. "Hey, Jimmy!" I caught up with him just past the fork in the road.

"Hey, Will. Where've you been?"

"I had to take Sarah back to Aunt Fran yesterday. Can't believe what happened!" I spent most of the rest of the way to school telling him about Lt. Davis and Mr. Jake and my job for the next day. "A whole dollar, Jimmy! Why don't you come with me? Maybe Mr. Jake would hire you, too."

"Sure would like to, Will. I can only get to school now though. Pa's real sick, and I've got to be around to help as much as I can. I'm afraid he's going to die, Will, just like I saw miners do when we were in Pennsylvania."

I tried to make him feel better. "Maybe it's just 'cause of the winter cold he's feelin' bad. Bet he'll be better in the spring."

"Sure hope so," was all Jimmy said.

Before we started our reading lesson, Mrs. Wilson asked, "William, since you've been to Charleston so often, what do you know about this new country that will be forming soon?"

"New country? I thought South Carolina was its own country now."

"Perhaps. But other states have seceded as well, and there is talk about having all seven band together."

"Yes, ma'am," Jimmy interrupted. "I know some about that. Grandpa is so excited about it, he buys a newspaper whenever he can. Maybe I could bring them to school so we could read about it."

"That would be nice. But can you tell us what you do know, James?"

"As far as I know, delegates are meeting in Montgomery. They want to start a new country called the Confederate States of America. It's sort of the same way the United States started, only this time, there wasn't a war. The last paper Grandpa got said they were working out how the government would work. They don't want a government that can tell the states what to do."

"Thank you, James. So it sounds like we will all be living in another country even though we haven't moved. That could be very interesting."

"Grampa says it's time to let the people live like they want to live."

"What other states would be in this new country?" I asked.

"I think it's Georgia, Florida, Alabama, Mississippi…and I forget the other ones."

"That sounds like a lot of the South. Do you think it'll work, Mrs. Wilson?"

"We'll have to wait and see, William. Right now, I'd like you to read the first page of the book you brought and write any new words on the board for the others to see." Class had started.

• • •

I hardly slept that night. I was excited and a little scared about going to Fort Sumter. It had looked so big when we passed it going to Morris Island that I was sure I could get lost in it if I had to carry supplies in. I was excited to see Lt. Davis there and hoped we had time for him to show me around some.

I don't think I had slept long when Pa shook me. "Better get goin' if you're goin' to keep that promise. I don't want you stoppin' nowhere on your way home. Don't go see Sarah. You get back here soon's you can. I ain't goin' to have a minute's peace 'til I see you safe."

I rolled out of bed, put on my clothes, and ate a little of the bread and jam that was left. I drank some milk and was on my way out the door when Pa said, soft-like, "You come home safe, you hear me, boy? I love you, and you belong here. Guess you're comin' on to bein' a man."

"Yes, sir." I sort of stuttered it. It ain't like Pa to talk like that. It made me think a little about how close we were. "I love you, too." I closed the door.

It was still dark, but clear, and pretty cold. I was glad I remembered to take my jacket. I knew it was always colder out in the harbor. Something about the air comin' off the cold water.

I got to the dock just as first light was comin' into the harbor from the ocean. It looked like Mr. Jake had just gotten there.

"Will, glad you made it this early. We can get loaded and get moving out with the tide."

Just then, Tom came by and asked with his hat in his hand, "Mr. Jake, you got any work for me today?"

"Sure do, Tom. Good to see you. I'm takin' a load of provisions out to Fort Sumter. I could use your help."

Tom paused. "Sorry, Mr. Jake. Last time we went that way, we was caught in shootin'."

"Come on, Tom. I'll pay you fifty cents cash when we get back."

I was going to say something, but Tom beat me to it. "Fifty cents! Sure will help. Guess I can duck if'n I need to!"

"You go over there and start with that crate, Tom."

When Tom was far enough away so he couldn't hear me, I said, "But, Mr. Jake, you said a dollar was the rate, and Tom can haul heavier crates than me."

"A dollar for a white man. Fifty cents for a black one."

"It doesn't seem fair."

"If you don't think it's fair, I can pay you fifty cents, too. Would that make you happy, Will?"

"No, sir. Which crate do you want me to load first?" I turned away and got to work.

We were loaded and on our way with the tide. The sky was light, but the wind in the harbor was cold. I crouched down to get out of it when I could. A cup of hot milk would be real good right now.

We came around to the pier that ran off the gorge wall of the fort. It was the longest wall and the one that we had passed to get to Morris Island. I noticed more cannons mounted at the fort than I did the first time we were there. I don't know if I hadn't paid attention or if they were getting ready for something.

When we landed the boat, a sentry told us to stop and identify ourselves. He looked edgy and stood there moving his rifle from one hand to the other. Tom slunk down, and I was getting more scared than I was before.

"Private!" The shout came from behind the sentry. He spun around and saluted. It was the lieutenant. "Private Hough, no need to stop these men. They are the ones I hired to bring the provisions." That was the second time I had been called a man that morning. It was funny, because I didn't feel no different than when I was a boy yesterday.

"Yes, sir!" the private snapped. "Shall I help them unload?"

"Good idea, Private." Behind the lieutenant was someone else in a fancier uniform.

"Yes, sir, Major!" The private began to help us unload the crates and barrels from the boat.

"Major Anderson," said Lt. Davis, "this is Will McShane. It's because of him that we got these supplies here today."

The major walked over to me and held out his hand. "I'd like to thank you personally, Will. The men will appreciate these supplies. I'd also like to thank the both of you." He looked at Mr. Jake and Tom. "OK. Let's get some more help to unload this. Lieutenant, get some of the workers out here to give these men a hand."

We had been stacking everything onto the pier, and it was all going pretty quick. I guessed I was not going to see the inside of the fort. I had an idea. "Major, should I carry this into the fort?"

"That won't be necessary, Will," said Major Anderson. Then he looked at me and changed his mind. "Yes, that would be a good idea. I'll show you where to put it." He smiled at the lieutenant.

I was sort of nervous about going with a major. He was in charge of everything here. The box seemed to be getting heavier with each step, and I was praying I wouldn't drop it. "How would you like to take a look around while you're here, Will?" the major asked.

"Yes, sir!"

"Put the box there and follow me. I don't think they will mind if you spend an extra few minutes."

The fort seemed bigger on the inside. The walls must have gone up to the sky. Three sides had what looked like lots of rooms, and two walls had lots of holes in them, looking like cannons would fit there real good. There were lots of the big guns lined up in the middle, laying on the ground.

"Those are the barracks, Will. They were built for hundreds of men and officers. We only have about eighty-five here now. Take a look at the other walls. Those three levels of the fort are intended for cannons. We have a few mounted, but not many. Most of our workers have left, so we are moving slowly at getting things ready."

"Ready for what?"

"I'm not sure, Will. The fort was built to protect the harbor. Now I don't know what will happen. All I know is that we are United States soldiers here, and this is a federal fort. It is my duty to defend it."

"Against what?"

"Well, we were supposed to defend the harbor against the Spanish or the British, maybe the French if they had any ideas about attacking. You know, Charleston is a very important port. Other countries would love to control it. I'm not sure what will happen now. I wait for orders from Washington and try to do what I can to make this a useful United States fort."

"Some people say there will be a war. Is there goin' to be a war?"

"I certainly hope not. I've been in a war, and it is terrible. I don't want to be in another one. I've been doing everything I can to help avoid a war."

"Will! Let's get a move on!" It was Mr. Jake. He had come through the sally port to find me.

"Thank you, sir," I said to the major over my shoulder as I ran out.

Major Anderson followed us to the boat. Before we shoved off, he looked at Tom and asked, "How would you like a job here? We could use some extra help, and the pay is good."

Tom hardly got his mouth open when Mr. Jake said, "He ain't gonna stay. I brought you food; I ain't helping Yankees get guns ready to fire at us. You ain't stayin', Tom."

"Yes, Mr. Jake." After he said that, I wondered how free a freedman really was.

• • •

By the time we docked back in Charleston, I was more confused than I had been about why everybody was in such a state about the fort. It was sure big, but it seemed mostly empty. The major had told me how few soldiers were there, and the South Carolina regiment and the Citadel had hundreds.

"Will!" Mr. Jake caught me up short when I was walking off the boat. "Your dollar! Can I count on you if I do this again?"

"Don't know. Maybe." I looked at Tom, who was looking down at the coins in his hand. "See you, Tom." He only nodded.

I made it home fast as I could to put Pa's mind at ease. He was in the shed, tending to Gray's hooves. It had been pretty wet and muddy, and horses hooves can get soft. If that happens, the horse can't work. "Glad you're back," said Pa. "How'd it go?"

I started talking, and words and questions came spillin' out of my mouth. I told him about meeting Major Anderson and seeing the inside of the fort and about Tom's pay being only fifty cents and Mr. Jake not letting Tom stay to work if he had wanted to.

"Slow down, Will. Sounds to me like you're learnin' a lot about what's goin' on in Charleston and a lot about how different people are treated." He bent down to pick up his tools and said, "I'm about done here. We're goin' to work on getting the field ready. Have to start plantin' soon."

We worked 'til sundown. While we were eating dinner Pa was talking about the Jockey Club races the next week. I had forgotten about them because of everything else that was happening.

"Remember last year, when Fran made a picnic lunch for us and we all went?"

"Yes, Pa. Can we go again? Maybe Jimmy could come with us."

"You can ask him if you want to. We'll probably be going with the Caldwells, too. One more won't make any difference. It will be a full wagon. We can bring Sarah back with us. How does that sound?"

I nodded, but I was getting too tired to say much. It had been a long day and a lot of work.

"You get to bed, son." He didn't have to tell me twice.

● ● ●

At school the next day, I told Jimmy about the races and that everybody would go. Besides the races, there were big dinners and grand balls. We never went to those, but the races and picnics were lots of fun. "Last year, we pretended we had a lot of money and made pretend bets. I won a pretend thousand dollars!"

"Grampa's been talking about it for two weeks now. I know he wants to go. I can see if I can go with you, or maybe just meet up with you there. I'm pretty sure my folks won't be going. My pa is getting sicker instead of getting better."

I was sorry to hear that. I hoped Jimmy could go so he wouldn't have to think about his pa, at least for a little while.

CHAPTER 12

• • •

"Let's get goin'. I'm sure all of the Caldwells will be waiting for us." Race day was finally here.

We hitched Gray to the wagon and headed down the road to their farm. We were going to drive them to town, pick up Sarah and Aunt Fran, and go to the races.

When we got to their place, sure enough, they were all ready to go. I had seen them a few times passing by as they went to town but didn't know them well. Dirk was the oldest. He was the one that had a bad arm. Jacob was about nine years old. He was tall and skinny but had a big smile on his face. I could tell he was ready to go. Rhett was the youngest. I don't think he really knew where we were going. He stayed close to his ma.

Mrs. Caldwell carried two big baskets with her to the wagon. I wasn't sure if I would have fun with all these folks, but I was sure I would eat good today.

Ridin' into town, I got to know the Caldwells a little better. Mrs. Caldwell seemed like a nice lady, but she was pretty stern. Guess with three boys and no husband, a woman would have to be. Rhett didn't say nothin'. He sat by his ma in the seat between her and Pa and held on to her hand the whole way there, like he was scared of us. Dirk didn't talk much either. I had noticed that when he helped Mrs. Caldwell into the wagon and lifted a basket of food, he did it with one hand. He probably couldn't use the other one. Jacob chattered all the way to town. I suppose he was the most excited about the races and the picnic. It was probably good for all of us to have a break from the farm for a day.

Ridin' into town took longer than usual. There were a lot of wagons on the road, lots of people on horseback, and lots walkin'. Everybody was goin' to the races. I think all of Charleston shut down for this, 'cause it looked like everybody was headed there.

We were able to get down Meeting Street to the Hawkins' to pick up Aunt Fran, but it took some doin'. Glad Pa was payin' good attention, because a little boy ran in front of the wagon. He pulled Gray back so quick I think it surprised the poor old mare, but we missed runnin' into the boy.

Aunt Fran, Sarah, and Miss Annie were waiting for us when we got there. There was another big basket of food between them. Pa was looking back into the wagon that already had four of us in back plus two big baskets. "Poor Gray," I heard him whisper.

"This is goin' to be crowded, Fran."

"Don't worry, John. We are waiting for Joseph to bring the buggy around. We will ride with him and meet you there."

"Want to go with Willie!" squealed Sarah as she headed toward our wagon.

"That's fine, Sarah. We have room for you."

Dirk was sitting closest to the back of the wagon. He jumped down, and with his good arm, he picked up Sarah and hoisted her into the wagon and then got back in himself. "Thanks, Dirk," I said.

"That was easy. She's as light as a feather."

We were on our way when Joseph pulled up with the buggy and helped the ladies in. I turned to see Terrance lift the basket on and then jump on himself. Everybody was going to the races.

• • •

The park was crowded with wagons and picnic blankets laid out. Even with all the folks there, it didn't take long to find Jimmy and his grandparents, Mr. and Mrs. O'Rourke. I was glad he could come and hoped he would have fun today.

While the grown-ups got the blankets and baskets down, Jimmy and I decided we would see what was going on. Pa suggested, "How 'bout takin' the other boys with you, Will?"

"Sure, Pa. Come on." Dirk shook his head, and Rhett held his ma's hand tighter, but Jacob jumped up and was ready to go.

Sarah cried, "Me, too. Want to go with Willie!"

"Not now, Sarah. We would really like you to stay here and watch the races with us and help us get the picnic lunch set for everyone."

"Goody. Races and picnics."

"Thanks, Mrs. Caldwell." The three of us were off.

It didn't take long for us to find a crowd of boys playing a game with a ball and a stick. Someone would throw the ball toward the boy with the stick, and he would try to hit it. If he did, he would run as far as he could in a big circle before somebody got the ball and tagged him with it. I asked if we could play, and they said sure. I noticed Jason Wilson and his brother in the game.

I looked at Jacob. "Do you think Dirk would play?"

"No. He don't do nothin' since his arm ain't right."

"I'll be right back." I ran back to where Pa and Mrs. Caldwell were puttin' down our things. Mr. and Mrs. O'Rourke were joinin' us. "Dirk, come play ball with us!"

"Can't. Gotta help my ma."

"It's all right, Dirk. There is plenty of help here," said his ma.

"Can't. My arm don't work."

I tried once more. "How about your other arm? Can you throw the ball?"

"Maybe."

"Come on and try it. Bet you can do it." He followed me slowly, looking back at Mrs. Caldwell, who was smiling and nodding. Terrance followed, too.

"Can I play, Mr. Will? I can run after the ball."

"I guess so, Terrance."

We told Dirk he should be the thrower. That way he could use his good arm and not have to try to catch. He wasn't sure at first, but after he tried it a few times, it seemed to be working fine.

We played until we heard Aunt Fran call us. They had all the food set out on the blankets. I don't think I'd ever seen so much in one place before. There were piles of fried chicken and thick slices of ham to put on lots of fresh bread. We ate cold cooked potatoes that were mixed with other vegetables. There were biscuits to put Mrs. Caldwell's blueberry preserves on. The sweet-potato pie tasted better today than it had the first time I ate it.

We were all just about groanin' from being so full but kept eatin'. When we slowed down, I heard Miss Annie tell Aunt Fran, "I wish my brother could have been here."

"Where is he, miss?" It was Mr. O'Rourke.

"Oh, he's at the fort and certainly can't travel around Charleston easily."

"Fort Moultrie is pretty far away."

"No, sir. He's at Fort Sumter."

"Sumter! He's a Yankee?"

"Well, sir, he is in the United States Army. He is Lieutenant Jefferson Davis."

"Ain't possible! Jefferson Davis was just elected president of the Confederate States of America. I got the newspaper here to prove it!" I could tell Jimmy's granddad was getting worked up.

"I can tell you,"—her voice was getting a little louder—"my brother would certainly not be president, because he is in the United States Army! He will continue to serve the United States!" Miss Annie's face was gettin' real red.

"He would certainly not be president because we wouldn't elect no damn Yankee!"

"O'Rourke!" It was Pa. "There will be no cursing in front of the ladies!"

"Sorry, ma'am. Miss."

"Joseph, maybe it's time we went home." Miss Annie started packing things in the basket.

"Are you happy now, Sean?" Jimmy's grandma asked. "You've upset her."

"Didn't mean to upset nobody. Just sayin' my piece. Cut me another slice of that chocolate cake, Thelma."

The conversation was over, but the mood was very different now. Seemed everybody was afraid to talk. I asked Dirk and Jimmy if they wanted to go back and play ball. "Jimmy can't go," said Sean O'Rourke. "We gotta be gettin' back to see about his pa." I guessed his grampa had the final say on everything. "I don't really trust that woman to care for him proper."

"She ain't 'that woman.' She's my ma, and she takes care of him fine!"

"Don't backtalk me, boy. Help your grandma get these things into the wagon, and let's go."

"Jimmy can come back with us," Pa suggested. Maybe everybody could calm down better if they were apart for a while.

"Don't make no nevermind to me. Do what you want to after you load the wagon."

"I'll go back with you, Grampa."

Mr. O'Rourke had a little bit of a smirk on his face.

"He certainly is an unpleasant man," said Mrs. Caldwell after he left. "I wouldn't mind not meeting up with him again. Boys, do you want to watch the races or play ball?" We decided to watch some of the horse races. We were really too full to run around much.

Pa said, "Sarah, you can come sit with us now."

"No. I want to sit here." She was sitting so close to Mrs. Caldwell, she was about on her lap. Rhett was there next to her. They looked like they had a game going on between them, and they were giggling when Rhett pretended that Dolly was talking. Even after all the tea parties we had, I never thought to make Dolly talk.

After we took the Caldwells home, Pa asked, "Did you like them?"

"Sure, Pa. I liked them well enough. Sarah seemed to be having a good time with them." She was sound asleep in my lap on the wagon seat.

"She did."

"Pa?"

"Yes, Will?"

"Oh, nothin'." I wasn't sure I should ask what I wanted to ask.

"Can't be nothin'. What?"

"Um, we goin' to be seeing the Caldwells more?"

"I expect so. They're goin' to need help planting."

● ● ●

Jimmy wasn't in school for the next few days. I guessed it was to help out since his Pa was so sick. The day he did come, he said it was only to tell us all that he wouldn't be coming anymore.

"Was your grampa so mad he won't let you come to school?" I asked.

He hung his head, and I saw a tear drop from his face. "My father died."

"Oh, James, I'm so sorry." It was Mrs. Wilson. She came over to him and put her arm around his shoulders.

"Funeral's tomorrow at ten o'clock." He was out the door before anybody could say anything else.

We were all pretty quiet when I said, "Mrs. Wilson, I don't guess I feel too much like learnin' today. Is it all right with you if I go home to tell Pa?"

"Of course, William. I know you and James are good friends and I'm sure this must bring back memories for you, too."

"Yes, ma'am."

I left and trotted down the road to try to catch Jimmy. It didn't take long. He was walkin' real slow. "Jimmy, wait up." He stopped but didn't turn around. "Feel like talking? I know how bad it hurts."

He nodded but didn't say nothin'. We walked a ways. Then he started cryin'. "Will," he sort of was sputterin', "Pa dying is bad enough, but Grampa just keeps yellin' about how it's Ma's fault. It isn't her fault, Will. She took care of him."

I didn't know what to say for a while, then I remembered what the pastor told me at Ma's funeral. "It ain't never nobody's fault because somebody is sick and dies. Pastor told me that maybe God wanted my ma because she was so good. Maybe God wants your pa because he was a good person, too."

"I don't want God to have him! We need him! God's got enough good people!"

I didn't say anything else. I remembered feeling the same way. I blamed God. I blamed Pa. For a while, I even blamed Little Sarah for being born. I still don't know why Ma had to die, but I know it was nobody's fault. I figured Jimmy would know that sometime soon, but today was too soon. He turned at the fork in the road without another word.

Pa was surprised to see me home so early until I told him what had happened. "I'm goin' to the funeral tomorrow, Pa."

"Of course. So am I. I'll see if Mary Caldwell could look after Sarah for a few hours, because she's too young to go. You take Sarah fishing for a while. I'll ride Gray over to the Caldwells' and be back right away."

Sarah had fun running up and down the bank, waving her arms and yelling to the fish while we waited for Pa. He was gone longer than I guessed he would be, but I supposed that Mrs. Caldwell and Pa were both remembering. Sometimes I think it can make you feel better to remember those things with somebody else.

When Pa did get home, he told Sarah she would be going to see Rhett tomorrow and play with him while he and I went to see someone. She was excited to go and tried to get Pa to take her right then.

• • •

We took Sarah and Dolly to the Caldwells' the next morning on the way to the church. She was so excited, she was bouncing up and down the whole way and almost fell out of the wagon into Mrs. Caldwell's arms.

"Be back in a few hours, Mary."

"No hurry, John. I'm sure we will all have a good time while you are gone. I feel bad that I'm not going, but I never did meet Mrs. O'Rourke. I certainly wouldn't go to see Jimmy's grandfather. I would feel like a hypocrite."

"I understand. I will tell her you are thinking of her." Pa turned the wagon, and we were at the church real soon.

There weren't lots of folks there. Jimmy's family had only lived here a little while, so not many people knew them. All the Wilsons came, and a few people that seemed to know his grandparents. I think Jimmy was glad I was there. He sort of smiled at me while he held his mother's hand. His little sister, Janie, held her other one.

The service wasn't long, but the pastor said some nice words to us about how Charles O'Rourke was with God now and we should all be happy for him and the time we had here with him. Jimmy didn't look any happier, and I knew how he felt. No words made me happy after Ma died.

We were leaving the churchyard, saying good-bye to everyone and shaking hands. Mrs. O'Rourke was pleasant to everyone, but she looked real tired and sad. Janie clung to her mother like she was afraid if she let go, her mother might die and leave her, too.

Pa was shaking hands with Jimmy's grampa and sayin' something about helping out if he could when Mr. O'Rourke turned and glared at Jimmy's ma. "We wouldn't have to be askin' for help it weren't for that woman! She's the one who made him stay in that filthy coal mine 'til he got so sick, he died!" He was none too quiet about what he said.

Jimmy jumped between him and his mother and shouted back at him. "She isn't 'that woman'! She's my mother, and she didn't make him stay in the mine. She wanted him to quit, but he said no so he wouldn't have to come here and live with you!"

"Jimmy." It was his ma's quiet, calm voice. "Don't talk back to your grandfather. Everyone is upset today, and now is not the time or place to talk about this."

"That's right, boy. Don't you talk back to me after what I've done for you!" I could tell Jimmy was getting really mad. He was all red in the face but didn't say anything more. "Get in the buggy, Thelma. We're goin' home!"

"But, Sean, we need to wait until we thank everyone for coming." Jimmy's grandma sounded like a nice lady.

"I said to get into the buggy!"

"What about the others?"

"I'd like to stay until all of the guests have gone, Father O'Rourke," said Jimmy's mother.

"I said we're leaving. Come with us if you want to, or stay!"

I interrupted. "We can take you back if you'd like, Mrs. O'Rourke."

"Thank you, Will."

"That's settled. Now get into the wagon, Thelma!" Jimmy's grandma obeyed and tried to smile at everyone as she got into the buggy.

"I hate him!" whispered Jimmy. We were giving him, his ma, and his sister a ride back so they wouldn't have to walk. Mrs. O'Rourke, Janie, and Pa were in the seat, and Jimmy and I were in the back. I don't think they could hear us talking.

"You got to be nice to him, though. You're living there."

"Not for long. Ma wrote to her cousin back in Pennsylvania when Pa was getting real sick. He's got a farm there and some youngsters. Guess his wife up and left him and went off with a soldier somewhere. From what Ma said, she was young and didn't want to live on a farm in the middle of nowhere. So now, her cousin can use some help with the young ones, and I can help on the farm."

"Oh, Jimmy, I don't want you to move away."

"You're the best friend I ever had, Will. I don't want to move, either, but we have to. I'm not looking forward to living in a place where nothing happens. There's always something going on in Charleston."

"Where is it you're movin' to?"

"A little town called Gettysburg."

CHAPTER 13

• • •

IT GOT PRETTY QUIET AROUND our place after the funeral. Pa had taken Sarah back to Charleston, and Jimmy wasn't at school any more. It wasn't as much fun going, because I wasn't meeting up with him. I really liked having somebody to talk to. It was interesting for me to hear about how his mother felt about the soldiers and secession, too. I never figured people could think so different about things.

I was still learning a lot, and my reading was getting better. I had finished the book about the Revolutionary War and would have liked to get another one from Mr. Hawkins, but Pa and I were real busy getting the fields ready. Pa was spending more time at the Caldwells', helping them too, mostly when I was at school.

I was anxious to get the garden planted.

"Not yet, Will," said Pa. "I feel there might be a little more frost left in the winter."

"Pa, how about just the greens? I'll make sure they don't freeze."

"Don't know how you think you'll do that, but go on. You will be responsible to take care of them."

I planted a few rows, and then we got some rain. The greens came up quick, and I was feeling pretty proud of myself until the night it got so cold, they froze and died. Pa didn't say much the next morning when I saw what had happened. I said, "I got a dollar, Pa. I'll be heading into town after school to buy more seed."

"Good idea, Will. While you're there, stop in and see Sarah. Tell Fran that we're real busy with planting, but we'll come and get Sarah for a while after it's done."

"Yes, sir. I can take the book back and get another one, too. What do you think I should get?"

"Don't know for sure. Maybe Mrs. Wilson or Mr. Hawkins will have an idea."

At school, Mrs. Wilson suggested a book by somebody named Shakespeare but then thought that would be too hard for me to understand. Maybe I would like something about the French and Indian War, or I should think about asking if Mr. Hawkins had a book of poems. I was beginning to think that these were books that Mrs. Wilson would like me to get so she could read some of them, too. I wasn't much for poems.

I went to the market first to get the new seed. I sure would listen to Pa next time! I still had some of my dollar left, so I spent two cents to get Sarah some peppermint. It had been some time since I did that.

I walked by the dock to see what was happening there. People were moving around every which way. The big battery that they were building looked almost done. It was like a big, flat boat with one high side that had big windows in it. There were cannon carriages by each window, but no cannons yet. Behind the carriages, there were all sorts of boxes. I guessed they were for cartridges and shells. I couldn't figure how it was goin' to float once those cannons were mounted, and I couldn't figure out why they would need it anyway. Either the South Carolina regiment or the Citadel cadets had taken over Fort Moultrie, Fort Johnson, and Castle Pinckney, and a battery had been built on Morris Island. That seemed like more than enough to keep the eighty-five soldiers of Fort Sumter inside.

"Hey, Will!" It was Mr. Jake.

"Hey, Mr. Jake. How are you?"

"Busier than a bee. I'm needing help again. One of them soldiers came over the other day and was trying to get more provisions. Said he's got it all arranged except getting them out to the fort. When can you go out there with me?"

"Gosh, Mr. Jake. Pa wasn't happy about the last time I did that, and we got planting to do. Don't know if he'll let me do it again."

"Two dollars, Will."

"I'll be here Saturday early," I said as I walked away, wondering what I would tell Pa.

I was glad to see Sarah, and she was happy to have the peppermint. We went over to the park for a while and watched all the building over there. "What's that, Willie?"

"They're putting in big guns."

"Why?"

So she wouldn't get scared, I said, "To keep you and everybody else safe." That seemed to answer her question, and she went back to eating her peppermint stick.

"Oh, Will—there you are!" Miss Annie called from across the street. She walked up to us. She was all in a whirl again about her brother. "Jeff was hoping I would see you. He asked me to tell you the men really are in need of the foodstuffs that were ordered, and he knows that the boat captain won't go out there without you. You have to help them and take the food to them. I'm afraid they will get sick from malnutrition because their supplies are so low, and there doesn't seem to be a supply ship coming to help them. They aren't getting any orders from President Buchanan either. I hope that after Mr. Lincoln is inaugurated, they can all go home."

"I did see Mr. Jake this mornin'," I told her. "I'm plannin' to help him on Saturday—unless Pa won't let me."

"Oh, Will, your father mustn't stop you. Please beg him if you have to. I'll beg him if it will help. They must have food!"

"I'll tell him what you said, Miss Annie. It might be easier to convince him if he knows how upset you are."

"Thank you, Will. I was going to see if Sarah and you would like to come back to the house for a snack before you left, but I see Sarah already has hers."

"I 'spect peppermint is her favorite food, but I'll come over to see what good things Aunt Fran has cooked up. I want to get another book, too. Do you have any ideas for one?"

"What about something about science and nature?"

"Good idea. Maybe I can learn about how Pa knew not to plant the garden too early." She looked at me like she had a question. I explained what had happened about the seeds and the plants freezing, patting my bulging pocket.

She smiled and nodded. "Yes, I expect he would know." We crossed the street to see what treats Aunt Fran had created for us and to find a book about science.

• • •

"Yes, Pa. I know I was supposed to ask you first, but Mr. Jake said two dollars! I could make a lot of money if I just stayed around the dock and worked there."

"You ain't stayin' around the dock, and you ain't makin' a lot of money! You hear me, boy? I don't want you mixed up in this mess anymore! You ain't goin'!"

I tried to be calm and hoped Pa would simmer down. "Pa, you know how scared Miss Annie is about her brother. This is to help her out as much as it is all of those men at the fort. She was talking about malnutrition because there wasn't a supply boat comin'."

Pa did calm down. "Yes, I do like her, and I know she's all aflutter because of her brother. That doesn't mean you have to be the one to get hurt—or worse—takin' supplies to the Yankees. 'Sides, they're in a foreign country now, and they weren't invited. Sooner they're gone, the better."

"I know that, but we can't let 'em starve while they're waiting to leave. Please, Pa."

He was quiet for a long time. "This is the last time, Will. I don't care how much he's payin' you, you will not go again! Do you understand that? If I have to, I'll go down there and tell them all you can't help no more!"

"Thank you, Pa. When I go on Saturday, do you want me to bring Sarah back with me? If she can't walk all the way, I can carry her some."

"Won't be no need to carry her. I've been working on a surprise for her, and it will help us, too. Come see."

Pa led the way to the shed and showed me a small wagon he made with a handle you could pull. "I figured if she's going to be around here a lot, we'll need to have a way to get her around so we can plant and such and not have to carry her. Take this with you, and bring her back. Mary—I mean Mrs. Caldwell—invited us to Sunday dinner. I know Sarah would want to go, and little Rhett gets along real good with her."

• • •

I left especially early on Saturday so I could get the wagon to the Hawkins before I helped Mr. Jake. I didn't want to leave it at the dock because I was pretty sure it wouldn't be there when I got back. Aunt Fran was already bustling around the kitchen. "Here, Will. Take this fresh bread and jam to eat on your way to the dock. I'll have Sarah ready when you get back. I hope it won't be too late. Although the days are getting longer, I don't want you to be walking home in the dark."

"I'd be all right. I've done it before."

"I know. But things aren't the way they were before. Now hurry on."

Mr. Jake and Tom were loading the boat. I was surprised to see Tom there but didn't say nothin' but good morning to both of them. When Tom walked down to the end of the dock to get the last of the supplies, Mr. Jake said, real quiet, "Don't say nothing about the two dollars, Will."

"No, sir." I figured it was between them, and I didn't need to get into the middle.

We got to the fort after a long while because the tide was just turning to come in. There was enough of a breeze to help, but it was slow.

Some of the soldiers were there waiting for us. I guessed they were happy to get those supplies. There were lots of men, and they were having to work hard getting the fort finished and cannons in place. I expected they could use a lot of food.

Lt. Davis, Pvt. Hough, and a few others got us tied up to the wharf in no time. "Good to see you again, Will, Jake, Tom. We appreciate you bringing these provisions out to us."

"I ain't doin' it for appreciation. I'm doin' it for the pay!" Mr. Jake snapped.

"I understand, but I appreciate it all the same. Hough, Pinchard, get these things unloaded so these men can get back and you can get back to work and Cook can bake us some bread." The two privates nearly jumped onto the boat to follow orders.

"Private Hough, can you help me with this?" I asked.

"Nobody calls me that but Lieutenant Davis and the major. My name is Daniel. I like that better."

"I'll call you Daniel, or anything you want me to call you, if you'll give me a hand." He chuckled and bent over to pick up the crate by himself.

We had made a lot of trips up and down the wharf and into the fort. It didn't take long with all the help they were giving us, but I noticed that Tom was moving slower than usual. On one of his trips, he had been in the fort for a long time. After everything was off the boat, Mr. Jake yelled to him to get aboard so we could catch the tide.

"No, sir. I ain't goin'."

"What?" screamed Mr. Jake.

"Said I ain't goin'." Tom repeated. "I'm staying here to work for the soldiers. They goin' to pay me a fair wage."

"Don't believe them. They won't pay you. They're Yankees, and you can't trust 'em."

"Seems like they pay you, and you trust 'em."

Mr. Jake was getting more agitated. "That's 'cause I'm white. You ain't—or hadn't you noticed?"

"That's enough, Jake," Lt. Davis broke in. "You heard him. He's not going back with you. If you are going to take advantage of the tide, I suggest you leave this minute."

"I won't be helping no damn Yankees no more!" Mr. Jake was all red and huffy. "Try to be good to them, and they steal my man."

"I ain't your man! I'm free, and I'm my own man." I'd never heard a black man talk like that before, and I wanted to cheer for Tom, but I kept quiet. I still had to go back with Mr. Jake.

It was a real quiet trip back to the city. I was glad for Tom, and it didn't bother me about no more supply trips to the fort, because Pa wouldn't let me go anyway. When we got to the dock, Mr. Jake gave me my pay, and I walked away, hoping I never had to see him again.

• • •

I was glad I was walking home with Sarah. She always makes me smile. The wagon worked pretty well as long as she would sit in it, but she would get to wriggling around and want to get out. She'd walk a little and then want to get in. It went slowest when she decided she should give Dolly a ride and pull the wagon herself.

Pa was waiting for us when we got home. "I was starting to worry. What took you so long?"

"Sarah liked to pull the wagon instead of ride in it," I answered.

He smiled. "Let's get supper and it's to bed early. We're going to start working hard on getting some of the cotton in. I want to get over to help the Caldwells, too. Sorry, Will, but I think you won't be goin' to school for a while."

"Yes, sir." I knew that was the agreement we had made, but I didn't really like it much. Guess I would get back to it when the planting was done.

After we had Sarah in bed, I told Pa what had happened with Mr. Jake and Tom.

"That does it, Will. You ain't goin' with him again! I don't trust a man who treats people like you told me he treated Tom. I don't care that Tom is black. He is free. You stay away from Jake. He's trouble!" That was the end of the discussion and I knew better than to ever bring it up again.

CHAPTER 14

• • •

PA AND I TRIED REAL hard for two days to get the planting done, but it was really hard with Sarah there. She'd be real quiet for a while and play with Dolly and have her little tea party in the wagon, but there would be times we would turn around and she was gone. We would have to stop what we were doing to go find her, bring her back, and try to keep her busy while we worked.

The second day, Pa decided we couldn't go on that way. That was after we found Sarah at the river. "Go fishing, Willie?" She smiled.

Pa had been getting pretty mad, but he could only smile back at her. "Not today, Sarah. Today Will has to help me."

That night Pa told me I needed to take Sarah back to Aunt Fran until planting was through.

"What about Mrs. Caldwell, Pa? Could she watch Sarah during the day?"

"It would be nice, but they got their own work to do. Sarah needs to have somebody watching her all the time and we can't do that right now."

• • •

We were off early the next morning. Pa let me take Gray and told me to get back as quick as I could.

"Morning, Aunt Fran." We were a bit of a surprise to her. She thought Sarah would be with us for a while.

"Oh, Will. What are you doing here?"

"Pa says we can't watch Sarah while we plant, so I needed to bring her back 'til we're done."

"Oh, dear." I could tell she was in a state. "Well, we'll have to make do. Annie may have time to watch her."

"What about the servants?"

"We are all scrambling, Will. The Hawkins have decided to hold a big 'non-inauguration ball' in honor of Lincoln not being our president. He'll be inaugurated in Washington next week, so we have to get everything ready by then. They have invited most of Charleston. The Hamptons, the Pinckneys, the Middletons, the Draytons, and on and on. And if that isn't bad enough, supplies in town are hard to come by. With all the soldiers that are moving in, it's getting harder to find extra food."

She stopped to take a breath and her face brightened up. "Will, can you help? How much butter and eggs can you get? Can you do some fishing and maybe hunting to get us a little more food for all of these people?"

"I don't know, Aunt Fran. We're pretty busy with planting, but I can ask Pa."

"Thank you, Will. I need as much as you can do by the end of the week. I know Mr. Hawkins will pay well for all of it."

"We most certainly will help her!" Pa made up his mind when I told him about Aunt Fran's problem. "She has been so good to Sarah and to us, we will do what we can if we have to work twenty-four hours a day. It's only for a few days. Let's figure out a plan so we can get as much planting done as possible and get in some fishing and hunting." Somehow, I knew part of this plan was going to have me churning the butter.

The first few days, we took turns at planting and hunting. The meat could hang for a time while we fished. Sure as I figured, it was my job to do the churning at night. That was something I could do in the dark. By the end of the week, we were tired to the bone but had a good supply of meat, fish, butter, and eggs loaded in the wagon. We decided both of us should go to town. We needed the rest.

• • •

"I can't thank you enough, John. I know Mr. Hawkins will pay you well for all of this."

"Glad I could help you out, Fran. You've done so much for us and Sarah. Where is she anyway? I'd like to see her before we go back to tell her she will be coming out to the cabin soon so she and Will can go fishing again."

"She's with Annie. That young lady has helped so much with Sarah this week. I don't know what I would have done without her. Poor girl. She's so worried about her brother. I know she's concerned about herself here too, but she doesn't dwell on that, only the lieutenant's safety. They may have gone across to the park, or what's left of it. Soldiers are digging up everything all over to put in batteries and piling up earthworks all over the city. Guess they figure it will be protection if Charleston is invaded by the Yankees."

"How can they invade? They only have eighty-five men"

"They may be worried about Yankee reinforcements or future invasions, Will. I don't know anything about war—and hope I never have to!" Aunt Fran was pretty stern about that part.

We found Sarah and Annie sitting on a bench with Dolly. It looked like Sarah was showing her where the guns were, because she would point to one, then look at her doll and do some talking.

"Hello, Miss Annie," said Pa. "I want to thank you for helping out with my little girl this week. We been workin' on gettin' things planted and had trouble keeping an eye on her."

"It has been no problem, Mr. McShane. Sarah is delightful and a good diversion. That way, I don't spend so much time thinking about all that is going on. There are rumors all over, and I don't know if I can believe any of them."

"Like what?" I asked.

"The Union troops are going back. The union troops are getting ready to attack. They are going to be resupplied. The Palmetto Guard is going to attack the fort. Those are just a few of the rumors. I have no idea what will be happening. I have only gotten a few short messages from Jeff. They mostly tell me not to worry but to be ready to leave at any time. Anyway, it has been wonderful having Sarah with me to take my mind off things. Maybe you will hear more when you go out there again, Will."

I looked at Pa. "I won't be goin' back, Miss Annie," I said real quiet.

"Oh, I see. I understand." She changed the subject. "Sarah, show your papa the new dress that we made for Dolly."

Sarah chattered on for a time while we walked back to the house. Annie asked, "When do you think you'll be coming to pick her up again, Mr. McShane?"

"We should be pretty well done in a few days. I'll have to help a neighbor out for a while, but Will and Mary—that's Mrs. Caldwell—will be able to keep an eye on her then. Why?"

"I was going to ask you if maybe I could come back with you for a short time."

Pa and I were both surprised. "Why would you want to come with us?"

"The Hawkins are having a big, fancy ball celebrating not having Lincoln for their president. All sorts of important people will be there. I think they are even going to invite the new general in charge, Beauregard. I don't think it would be good for anyone if I was around, but I think Mr. Hawkins would be offended if I hid in my room. I thought maybe I could tell him that I was going to help out with Sarah for a few days."

"Wouldn't matter to me none. But do you think it would be proper? People might get the wrong idea. Anyway, ain't you supposed to stay close by in case you have to leave in a rush?"

"I suppose you're right on both counts." She hung her head. "Maybe I'll just complain that I have a headache or something and stay away from their party. I do wish I could go home. This is all so unsettling."

"Don't fret, Miss Annie. It'll all work out." Pa sounded more confident about that than I felt after seeing all the cannons mounted along the battery. I hoped he was right.

When we went back to the house to say good-bye to Aunt Fran, she was sort of fidgety. "John, maybe I shouldn't ask," she started. "I know you have a lot to do at planting time, but I was wondering…"

"What is it, Fran?"

"Well, I was wondering if maybe Will might be able to stay here and help me out this afternoon and evening."

Pa was quiet for a time. He looked at me. "What do you think, Will?"

"I wouldn't mind helpin' out here," I said. I was thinking it would be a nice break from the kind of work we did last week.

"Fran, if he can help, then he can stay. It's the least I can do. Will, how about if I come back and pick you and Sarah up early tomorrow morning? Would that work for you, Fran?"

"That would be wonderful. There are so many little things that need to get done. Thank you, John. Thank you, Will."

If I was thinkin' I would get a break from workin', I was dead wrong. Aunt Fran had me all over town, carryin', totin', and pickin' up things for the big ball. By suppertime, I was pretty well tuckered out.

I put Sarah to bed and told her a story about a fish I caught one time that told me it was magic. It said that I could have three wishes come true if I let it go, so I wished for a big, new house, a big, new wagon with a new, young horse to pull it, and a new fishin' pole. "What happened?" she asked, real excited.

"Well, I let the fish go after I told it what I wanted and went home to look for the new house, wagon, and fishin' pole."

"Did you find them?"

"No, Sarah. The fish fooled me. There was nothin' different at home. But if I ever catch that fish again, I ain't lettin' it go!"

"Did you make that up, Willie?"

"I surely did. Now, you go to sleep. Tomorrow, Pa will pick us up to go back home. G'night."

"G'night, Willie. It's nice to have two places that are home."

I blew out the lamp and headed down to the library. I had asked Aunt Fran if I could look at the books and maybe take one home. She told me to look around and that she would send Joseph in to help me.

I had found a book about Daniel Boone. I'd heard about him and how he had taken settlers through the Appalachian Mountains. I got to wonderin' what it would have been like to be able to wander around the country and not have to be anyplace special. While I was lookin' at it, Joseph walked in.

"'Evening, Mr. Will. Did you find what you wanted?"

"I think so, Joseph. Thank you." He was leaving when I asked him, "Joseph, you told me you couldn't read very much. Why don't you read some of these books? There are so many of them, I'm sure Mr. Hawkins wouldn't mind."

"Maybe not, Mr. Will, but I don't want to cause no trouble for Mr. Hawkins. He's been too good to me."

"Why would that cause trouble? It doesn't seem to be any trouble for me to read them."

"Things are different when you're a slave. We couldn't learn how to read, or we were beat. Not by Mr. Hawkins—that was a long time ago, when I was a young one on a plantation. Some of the field hands tried to learn to read, and they got whipped bad. The master said readin' was against the law, and if he caught them doin' that again, he would take out one of their eyes so they couldn't see so good. It scared me enough to never want to read. I learned a few things from shoppin' in the market and such but never wanted no more of that kind of trouble."

"That doesn't make sense to me, Joseph. I would think that even if you were a slave, it would be better to be smart."

"Don't know about that, Mr. Will. I think some of the masters are afraid for slaves to know too much. If you don't know nothin', you have to believe what they tell you. It gives them the power. When you learn things, it gives you power."

"If Mr. Hawkins wouldn't mind, why don't you learn now?"

"Guess it's too late for me. I'm happy to be here. I'm gettin' on in years, and some masters will put you out when you get old. I wouldn't have no place to go." I was surprised to hear about that. He continued, "So I stay here and do what I can for Mr. and Missus Hawkins. They good people."

"Don't you have any family?"

"No, sir. About the time I was ready to get married, I got sold off to another plantation. I found a gal there I wanted to marry, but the master moved her into the big house and wouldn't let her marry a field hand."

"How did you get to be a butler?" I asked.

"I was gettin' older and got sold for cheap. I think Mr. Hawkins felt sorry for me. I been tryin' to make him happy for some time now. He's a good man. Now, I 'spect it's time for you to go to bed. You're lookin' tired, and I got a big day tomorrow. G'night, Mr. Will."

He was right. I was very tired. "G'night, Joseph."

CHAPTER 15

• • •

PA WAS THERE TO PICK us up early the next morning. Aunt Fran thanked us again for helping and for taking Sarah with us. The next day was the big party, and it was best if Sarah wasn't there to distract anybody from doing their jobs.

"You must have got up awful early to get chores done and get here for us, Pa."

"I did, son. We're not going right home. We're going to the Caldwells' for the day. I need to help finish things up for them."

"Go fishing, Willie!"

"Guess not, Sarah. Not today, at least. We're going to go to help Mrs. Caldwell, and I 'spect you can play with Rhett."

"Goody! Dolly wants to play with Rhett, too."

"That will be good, Sarah. How did you do at the Hawkins', Will?"

"Fine, sir." I told him about all the errands that Aunt Fran had me runnin' and that I had a little time to spend in the library. I told him about what Joseph had said to me. He just nodded.

I said, "I don't get why it's so hard to let people read. It could make their lives better."

"Will, knowledge is power, and the white folks don't want black folks to have any power. They're scared of that."

"That's what Joseph said. But I don't get what there is to be scared of."

"Think about it. These folks have been slaves, their parents and grandparents were slaves. Do you think they would let white folks do that to them if they started getting more knowledge?"

"Just because they know things doesn't mean they would have any power."

"I'm looking at you, Will. You want to learn. The more you learn, the more questions you ask. The more you ain't satisfied with the way things are. Am I right?"

I had to think about that for a minute, but then I agreed that he was.

"Well, if you ain't satisfied, how do you think thousands of black folks would act if they weren't satisfied?"

"Is that why there are laws about slaves reading?"

"Yes it is. Now, I have a question for you. It ain't what we been talkin' about, but I want to know what you think." I didn't know Pa cared about what I think, only what I did. "I been sort of plannin' to add a room on to the cabin for Sarah."

"I think that's a good idea, Pa."

"That ain't all. I thought it would be even better if we added on all the way along the back. That way, we could have three more rooms."

"Why do we need three more? One would be enough."

"Just thinkin' and plannin' a little. Three rooms wouldn't take all that much more work than one, and we'd have lots of space. We could each have a room."

"Sure, Pa, if that's what you want. I'll help you do it, one or three."

"Good. We can get started plannin' it tomorrow." Gray had brought our wagon up to the Caldwells' house. "Here we are," said Pa.

"Rhett, come catch Dolly!" Sarah squealed as she tossed the doll down only to see her get caught by the hair. She yelled at Rhett, "Don't pull her hair!"

He laughed. "Well, then, don't throw her!"

Mrs. Caldwell hoisted Sarah off the wagon with a big smile. "How's my Little Sarah?"

"I'm a big girl!"

"Yes, you are, and I'm so glad you could come to visit." That made Sarah feel important, and she, too, got a big smile on her face. "The other boys just headed out to the field to get started, John. Would you like some coffee before you go out there?"

"No, thanks, Mary. Will and I are goin' to see how much we can get done first. Hopin' we can get everything in today. Startin' to feel like rain."

"You go ahead, then. I'm going to get started on making a good dinner for all of us. Rhett will play out here with Sarah."

As we were walking out to the field, I said to Pa, "Why does Rhett have to stay so close to his ma? It don't seem right."

"We'll talk about it later. Now we have work to do. There are the boys. Let's see how far they are by now."

• • •

We worked hard for what seemed like a long time, and I was getting hungry—probably because I knew what a good cook Mrs. Caldwell was. We saw Rhett heading out toward us with Sarah skipping behind him. "Ma says dinner's ready!" he called out to us. "Says to tell you to wash and come in to eat."

"Thanks, Rhett," said Dirk. "'Bout time we got a rest."

Jacob and Pa were walkin' ahead of Dirk and me. "Thanks for all the help, Will. I know it's lots extra for you and your pa, but we really appreciate it."

"You been workin' pretty fair with one bad arm, Dirk. Looks like you'll be able to do it all in time."

"Don't know about that. It's gotten some better, but not much. Don't guess it'll ever be the same, but I've been learning that I can do an awful lot with my other arm. So it ain't so bad. I told your pa that I thought Jacob and I could finish this by ourselves in a day or two, but he insisted that he and you would come to help."

"I know Pa don't mind helpin'. Your ma likes Sarah, we all get along good. It's nice to have friends, and that's what friends do."

"Hurry on, you two! Dinner will be cold." Mrs. Caldwell was scoldin' from the door. "Didn't cook all morning so you could eat cold dinner!"

"Yes, ma'am," we both said at the same time and raced to the water bucket to wash the dirt from our hands.

• • •

All the hard work was worth it when I sat down to Mrs. Caldwell's cooking. There was plenty of pork, vegetables, and two sweet potato pies. I think I ate almost half of one myself.

"Well, Mary," Pa said between bites, "we'll be pretty well finished by the time we leave this afternoon. I'm sure Dirk and Jacob can do whatever we don't get done tomorrow."

"Sure can, Ma." It was Dirk. "Won't be no problem at all, Mr. McShane. Thanks for your help. We can try to get the rest of the garden in too, so long as it doesn't rain."

"You sure are doin' good, even with your bad arm, Dirk. Bet your ma is proud of you."

"I certainly am, John. He seemed so sad for so long, but just snapped out of it and was back to being himself right after we had the picnic at the races. I don't know what happened, but we are all glad for it."

Dirk looked at me and nodded. "Sometimes it takes somethin' special to know that you can still do good, even if it ain't quite the same as it was."

"All right, boys. Back to work." Pa pushed himself away from the table and headed for the door. We all followed. I looked back at Sarah who had been real quiet during dinner I saw her put her head down on the table. Guess she had a busy morning with Rhett.

It didn't take us as long as we thought it would to get most of the fields in. We got back to the house just as Sarah was waking up from a nap. "Well, Sarah, are you and Dolly ready to go home?" Pa asked her.

"Don't want to go. Play with Rhett!"

"No more today. We'll come back tomorrow. Mary said she and Rhett would watch you while Will and I did some work at home. We're gonna start a special project just for you. It will be a big surprise."

"*No!*" She crossed her arms and stomped her little foot. Mrs. Caldwell had to turn away so she didn't show Sarah the big smile on her face.

I tried next. "Sarah, Pa says we have to go, and there ain't no arguing with him. I'm lots bigger than you are, and I never tell him no. Let's go, and we'll come back tomorrow."

"*No!*"

Rhett was whispering in Mrs. Caldwell's ear and laughing at the same time. Mrs. Caldwell nodded. "Mr. McShane, if it is all right with you, can Sarah just stay here tonight? She will be happy, and you don't have to take the time to bring her back in the morning."

Pa hesitated and looked at Mrs. Caldwell. She smiled at him in a secret-like way and nodded. "Well, if you all think that's best. Would you like that, Sarah?"

"Yippee!" was the reply, and she took Dolly aside to tell her what they were going to do.

"But," said Pa sternly, "you will come home with us tomorrow night. Will or I will come to get you."

Rhett spoke up. "You won't need to do that, Mr. McShane. I'll bring her home."

"How will you do that?"

"It ain't a long walk, and we can have an adventure on the way down the road. Would you like that, Sarah?"

"Yippee!"

"Is all of this workin' for you, Mary?"

"That will be fine, John. It looks like all my boys are growing up."

• • •

As soon as we were out of the yard, I said, "Pa, why did you say yes to Rhett? He's such a mama's boy, he won't leave Mrs. Caldwell."

Pa thought for a minute. "You know, son, maybe he wasn't always a mama's boy, and maybe he won't always be one. You might not remember, but for a while after your ma passed, you wouldn't let me out of your sight. One day while we were eatin' dinner, you started cryin'. I figured you were sad about Ma and told you that she was with us and watchin' you grow up from a better place, so not to feel so bad. You told me you knew all that and you weren't cryin' because Ma was gone, you were cryin' because you were afraid I would leave you, too. It took you some time to figure out that I wasn't goin' anywhere. Rhett's daddy ain't been gone as long as your ma. Maybe he hasn't figured it out yet."

When I thought about it, I did remember feeling afraid Pa would leave me and I wouldn't know what to do. Now I understood how Rhett felt. I guess takin' care of Sarah was good for him. I guess that I was a little jealous, too, because she wanted to stay with him and not come with me. Maybe she wasn't sure where she belonged yet.

• • •

The next morning, Pa and I started planning for the extra rooms. Pa paced off the distances, and I put in stakes where he thought the rooms should be. "Ya know, Pa, this is pretty big. It's goin' to take a lot to cut down all them trees."

"We ain't cuttin' the trees. We're getting the wood delivered today from the lumberyard. It's cut and milled already, so our job won't be so tough."

"Pa! That's real expensive. Can we pay for all that?" I was pretty nervous about it all. Pa taught me never to buy nothin' unless you could pay for it so you weren't beholdin' to nobody.

"It's been taken care of, Will. I had some money saved up. What I couldn't pay cash for, I traded for."

"What we got to trade?"

"More wood. There's so much building goin' on that the lumberyard can use lots more than they got. They let me have the sawed wood in exchange for the stand of trees down by the river. They'll be comin' with equipment to cut and haul them away."

"By the river! Pa! That's where I do lots of the huntin'. That's where Sarah likes to run around and chase squirrels after we been fishin'. How could you give that away?"

He looked stern. "I didn't give it away. I sold it. There's other places to hunt and run around. We needed the wood, and I don't have time to chop it myself. Besides, with the trees down, it will be easier to clear so we can plant more crops."

I was confused, angry, and sad all at once. "Why do we need more crops? Seems like we have enough, and I'm not sure how two of us can manage more anyhow. More crops, bigger house? I don't get it, Pa. Why are you doing all this?"

He stopped what he was doing. "Come sit here, Will. I need to talk to you. I suppose I should have said something sooner, but I wanted to make sure it was really going to happen."

"What was goin' to happen?"

"I'm goin' to ask Mary to marry me, Will. We've talked about it some. She's a good ma to her boys, and she likes you and Sarah. You need a ma. Her boys need a pa. We've talked about how it might work, but I haven't really asked her yet. I want to have something to show her so she'll know that we can make all this work together. You got to admit, the cabin was a good size for two or three people, but not for seven."

I couldn't think of nothin' to say for a time. "Sarah needs a ma, Pa. I don't. Anyway, she could never take Ma's place for me."

"Will, I don't expect she will take your ma's place for you or for me. Nobody can take her place. That's fine. She'll never be the Sarah who gave birth to my children, but that don't mean she won't be good. I'm not looking for it to be the same as it was with your ma, and I wouldn't expect you to, either. I ain't plannin' on being the same kind of pa as Mr. Caldwell was to his boys. Just because it will be different don't mean it can't be good."

For a long time I thought I wanted a new mother so we could be a family with Sarah. I never thought about having three new brothers. It sure would be different. I didn't know if I liked the idea anymore.

Maybe Pa hadn't figured out some things. "Are seven of us going to fit in here, even with more rooms? Are we living on our land or hers? Are they goin' to call you Pa? What about Sarah? She's been through a lot. Won't this all be too much for her?"

"I know you have questions. I don't know all the answers, but I need you to trust me. I feel this will be good for all of us. Everybody will take lots of time to get used to this, but we all need to go on livin' the best way we can. I decided that I will ask her the next time we're together and hope she's thought it through enough to say yes."

I knew he was probably right. He usually was, but I couldn't help feelin' scared about havin' to share my pa. I swallowed hard and nodded, turned, and walked down to the woods to sit in my favorite place for the last time. Spike followed me like he knew there was something wrong. His head was down and his tail wasn't wagging like it usually did when we were headed for the river. I sat down on the bank, and he sat next to me so close that I was sure he knew he wouldn't be running through here no more and was sad about it, too.

I came here lots after Ma died. Sometimes I would try to talk to her. I would pray she would come back. I would cry. I would scream at God for taking her away from me. None of it made no difference, 'cept I had a place where I could do all that without nobody tellin' me not to cry or not to be mad at God. It was my place to be close to Ma, but it wouldn't be here no more.

CHAPTER 16

• • •

I DON'T KNOW HOW LONG I was sitting on the bank when I heard Sarah calling my name. I had thought a lot and cried some, but I knew Pa was right. It could be good, and we could make it work. "I'm here, Sarah. Is Pa with you?"

She and Rhett came through the trees. "No. Rhett's here."

"Hey, Rhett. Thanks for bringin' Sarah home." I didn't dare say any more, because I didn't know if Mrs. Caldwell had talked to him about getting married to Pa. Besides, she might even say no.

"We had adventure!" she chattered on. "We played we were Indians hunting for big tigers."

"Well, did you find anything?"

"Pine cones. I can throw far!"

"Good for you, Sarah. Did your ma come with you, Rhett?"

"No. She was helping Dirk and Jacob finish up in the field, so she told me to bring Sarah myself. Guess I should head back now. See y'all."

"Sure. Bye." He turned and walked away, whistling. I never saw him do that before. Maybe a marriage was going to be good for everybody else. I wasn't so sure about me.

• • •

Our new lumber was delivered the next day. I wasn't sorry about that, but I was sorry to see a wagonful of men head over toward the river and the stand of trees that I had spent so many hours in.

"Mr. Will!" I looked up into the wagon and saw Tom wavin' his hat at me.

"I thought you were working at the fort!" I shouted to him.

"Was, 'til I got really scared about all them guns. Got some pay and hitched a ride back on a supply boat..." By then, the wagon was out too far for me to hear him. I'd ask Pa if maybe Tom could help us do some buildin', like Old Joshua had.

Pa and I worked for the next couple of days while we listened to the saws and the men yelling "Timber!" and the trees crashing to the ground. It hurt a little every time I heard one go down. We were able to get the new rooms framed and one of the walls up even while watching Sarah. I think she was afraid of all the men, so she stayed close. I didn't tell Pa, but I was really glad we had all that cut and milled wood piled up. Guess you got to make trades for things you want.

When we got done working one night, Pa told me he would have to go to town for more nails. He thought a day of rest would be a good thing and I could go to school. It sounded like a good idea to me, 'cause I hadn't been there for so long. He would pick me up after school, and we would take Sarah back to Aunt Fran now that the big ball at the Hawkins' was done.

At school, Mrs. Wilson asked me if I had been able to do any more reading. I told her that we had been real busy with the planting and building, but I had been able to read some of the book I had gotten about the Revolutionary War. She asked me what I thought about it.

"Well, ma'am, I'm not too sure. I just don't get why people want wars. I think if the colonies and England would have sat down and talked about it, it could have worked out a lot easier than all that fightin'. They wanted to be free. Why not just let them?"

"That is an excellent question, William. I suppose you could say the same for the situation we are in now after secession. South Carolina, and now the other states, want to be separate. That's why they formed the Confederate States of America. So why doesn't the United States let them go and remove its army?"

I sort of could see how that was the same, but I could see how it wasn't, too. I knew the Confederate states had been part of another country. The colonies hadn't been part of England; they belonged to it just because England said so. If the Southern states wanted to be a separate country, why didn't they do it after the war with England instead of agreeing to be in the United States first? I think I was just getting mixed up more.

"That was quiet a long pause, William. You look confused. Shall we ask the others what they think?"

We spent our reading time talking about going to war or working things out peacefully. Even if we were all young, we had lots of different ideas, and Mrs. Wilson let us talk about them until she told us it was time for numbers. "I don't want you all to forget about your questions and ideas. Thinking of different ways to do things is good for you. If no one was thinking, the world would be in trouble. Now, let's review some long division."

• • •

"Hey, Sarah, Pa," I said when I jumped into the wagon after school. "Did you have a good morning? I did. We talked a lot about why people go to war and what they could do instead of killing each other."

"What's war?"

Pa gave me a long look that I took to mean I better not say another word. "Nothin' you need to worry about, Sarah. Will was just talking about school." He turned to me. "I have some news, Will. Sarah and I went to see the Caldwells this morning."

"I got to play with Rhett!"

"Please don't interrupt me, Sarah. While she and Rhett were playing, I asked Mary to marry me." He paused, and I couldn't say nothin'. It would be good for lots of reasons, but I guess I was sort of scared about so much changing. He continued, "She said yes. So it's all for sure now. Mary will be your new ma."

"My ma? Mary is my ma?" Sarah couldn't help but interrupt then.

"Not yet, Sarah. We have some things to do before that happens, but I think it will be soon. And remember that she is Mrs. Caldwell until then."

"How soon, Pa?" I asked.

"We'll go to church on Sunday and talk to the preacher. We got to get the house done, or at least most of it, and we have to figure what to do with the Caldwells' land. Not sure if we'll rent it or sell it. Lots of the rich folks keep buying up land for cotton. Our land's better, and we got more of it, 'specially when we clear it of trees. So we'll be keepin' all of ours and theirs for now."

More changes. Guess I would need to get used to it.

• • •

"Afternoon, Miss Annie. How are you today?" We met her in the garden on the way into the Hawkins' kitchen. Sarah ran to her and hugged her leg. Pa tipped his hat and went inside.

"I'm well, Will. I'm glad the big ball is over. It went better than I had hoped."

"Glad to hear it. Did you meet General Beauregard?"

"I made a point of it. I told him I was disappointed that South Carolina was treating one small garrison of United States soldiers as if they were an invading army. I said that I hoped cooler heads would prevail."

"Good for you. What'd he say?"

"We had a good conversation. He told me he had known Major Anderson at West Point when he was an instructor and the general was a student, and he had the utmost respect for the man. He knew Anderson was in a difficult position. They had sent communication back and forth, trying to work things out. No one wanted to start trouble."

"If nobody wants to start trouble, why is the harbor full of scout boats and bunkers and cannons being put all over?"

"We talked about that a little as well. He said it would have been possible to avoid war before, but Lincoln's inauguration speech the other day called for war."

"Lincoln wants war?"

"That's what General Beauregard seemed to think. Lincoln said a state cannot secede. The general said, 'We have, and it shall remain so!' He planned to keep negotiating with Major Anderson but was less hopeful every day. He also said he was sorry about my brother's position there and didn't want anyone to get hurt. He said he hoped that the major would withdraw his troops from the fort and go back to New York."

"Well, I sure hope he goes back, too, so we can stop all this fuss and get back to normal. Sure would hate to see you go back, though. I know Sarah would miss you, too."

"That's very sweet, Will."

Sarah had been tugging at Miss Annie's skirt since we got there but had not interrupted. "What is it, Sarah?"

"I got a new ma, Annie. Pa said so."

"What's this?"

"Pa's fixin' to marry Mrs. Caldwell. We been busy buildin' onto the cabin, and Pa got some land cleared so's we can plant more—because now there will be seven of us."

"My goodness, that is a big change. When will this all happen?"

"Don't know exactly. They'll be talkin' to the pastor on Sunday to see when he can marry them, and we're goin' to try to get more of the house done." I paused. "Guess it won't be a cabin no more."

"How do you feel about all this, Will?"

I looked down at Sarah, who had a big smile on her face. "Just fine," I said real quiet.

"I see." Miss Annie looked at Sarah, too. "Sarah, how about if you run inside and see if your Aunt Fran has a cookie for you?" Sarah must have thought it was a very good idea, because she raced toward the kitchen door without another word. "How do you feel?" she asked me again.

"I guess I like the idea. There's just goin' to be so many things different, it'll take time to get used to it all. I really like Mrs. Caldwell and her sons, but three brothers all at once seems like a lot. It'll be good to be able to have Sarah home all the time, and I'm pretty happy thinkin' about the food we'll be eating, too. Mrs. Caldwell is a good cook."

Miss Annie smiled. "I'm glad you like them all. It is important. Yes, give yourself time to get used to a whole, big family. I expect everyone will need time."

"Except for Sarah. It's good to see her so happy."

"I'll miss her. I hope I can come to the wedding."

"I guess you can. Probably won't be many folks there. Don't know what they're all planning."

"I'd like to go inside and congratulate your father."

Pa and Aunt Fran were sitting at the kitchen table. Sarah was on Pa's lap, with a cookie in her hand.

"Yes, John. I insist! You are my only relative, and I want to do that for you and Mary. I'm so happy that you have found someone. I know how hurt you were when Sarah died and what a hard time you and Will had. You deserve this. It will be wonderful to know you are all part of a family. Besides, I really like Mary. I'm happy for her, too. She's getting a good man."

"Sure wish you had found somebody, Fran."

"Well, that has been over for a very long time now. But that reminds me—I want you to have this." She pulled a ring out of her apron pocket and handed it to Pa. "It was Ma's, remember?"

"'Course I remember, but she wanted you to have it. I can't take it from you."

"Yes, you will, John. I'll never be able to wear it the way Ma wanted me to, and I think it should stay in the family. Maybe Little Sarah will have it one day."

"If you're sure about this, Fran."

I was thinkin' that getting married made people sort of funny. They were talkin' about bein' happy, but both Pa and Aunt Fran were wipin' their eyes.

"Don't you give it another thought. You have a ring, and you will have a small party after the wedding."

"I don't want you goin' to no trouble."

"It won't be any trouble," interrupted Miss Annie. "I'll help. May I?"

"Of course you can, Annie. Can't she, John?"

Pa smiled. "Didn't plan on this bein' a big to-do. Just a quiet wedding."

"It's settled."

"All right then, Fran. Will and me got to get to the market to get nails and a few other things so we can keep workin' on the house. I'll let you know what the preacher says and what Mary and I figure will be enough work done on the house before we know when this will be. I'm hopin' sooner rather than later. All right if you stay here with Aunt Fran, Sarah?"

"Annie too!"

"Yes," said Miss Annie. "Me, too."

• • •

We were leavin' the market with the supplies when I saw Tom walking down the road a little ways ahead of us. "Pa, how about we ask Tom if he could help us out?"

"That may not be a bad idea, Will." He hurried Gray on ahead to catch us up with Tom. When we got closer, he called out, "Tom! You remember me?"

He turned, and when he saw who had greeted him, he smiled. "Yes, sir." He took off his hat when he talked to Pa. "I remember Mr. Will, too. Nice boy. Good worker."

I smiled at him and said, "Thanks, Tom. Do you think you could come out to our place for a few days and help us out, buildin' on to our cabin? Pa's getting married pretty soon, and we need lots more space."

"Good for you, Mr. John. I'd be happy to help."

"I can't pay nothin' in money, but we got lots of eggs, and some of the vegetable garden is starting to get full. We could pay you mostly with that so's you could come back here and sell it."

"That'll be jest fine. 'Sides, I really like workin' with Mr. Will. He was good to me."

"See you tomorrow then, Tom." We were on our way home as Tom waved his hat.

I was real quiet goin' home, when Pa asked me if I was thinkin' 'bout the wedding. "No, sir. I was thinkin' that it's a little like havin' Old Joshua back with us. Do you think he knows I still think about him?"

"I'm sure he does, son."

CHAPTER 17

• • •

TOM WAS AT OUR CABIN early the next morning. "What do you want me to do, Mr. John?"

"We're goin' to have to cut at least one door in the back wall before we build those walls higher. This is where I'm plannin' to cut today. We'll need one more, but we can do that later. I want to get the outside walls finished and the roof on as quick as I can. Guess we need to start by puttin' in a hole, and then we can start sawing. Take this hammer and see if you can break through while I go out and work on it from the outside."

Just then, Dirk and Jacob showed up. "Good mornin', boys," said Pa, waving to them from the side of the cabin. "What brings you here so early?"

"Ma said we should come and see if we can help, since we're goin' be livin' here," Jacob said with a smile. Dirk wasn't smilin'.

"You sure can. The three of you can work on the short wall over there and see how high you can get it while Tom and me cut a door."

"Who's Tom?"

"He's a man I met when I took some supplies out to Fort Sumter a while back," I said. "With five of us workin', we can be done lots quicker than Pa and me thought. Come on, grab that end of the board."

"Lucky you could find somebody to work for you during planting season," said Dirk.

"Well, he's a freedman and ain't got no land, so I don't suppose he cares about plantin'," I answered.

"You mean you got a black man working here?" That's when I realized Dirk hadn't seen him yet.

"Sure. He's a good worker."

"Hope I don't have to work with him. I'll stay on the other side of the wall." I thought that was a strange thing to say, but I didn't answer.

We got to work. It wasn't long before we heard a loud crack and then the saw goin' back and forth. "Pa and Tom must've broke through the wall. They're makin' a door."

The three of us built up the wall as far as we could reach in the time it took Pa and Tom to cut the door. Tom walked through it to the outside and looked surprised to see Dirk and Jacob there. "Well, sir, who are these gentlemen?"

"This here is Dirk, and this is Jacob. They'll be livin' here with us after Pa and their ma get married."

Tom took off his hat and gave a little bow. He said, "Nice to meet you."

"Nice to meet you too, Tom." Jacob smiled at him. Dirk didn't say nothing, just mumbled under his breath.

"Well, with the door finished, looks like I can help you with that wall," said Tom. "Dirk, you're the tallest. You hold that board for me so's I can nail it in."

"Ain't no darky tellin' me what to do."

"Dirk!" Pa used a voice I didn't hear often. "Tom is helping us. He is our friend. You show some respect!"

"I don't need to show respect to the likes of him. You can't tell me what to do, either. You ain't my pa! Come on, Jacob. Let's go home."

"No, Dirk. Ma wanted us to help, and I'm stayin'."

"Suit yourself!" Dirk yelled back over his shoulder as he was walkin' down the path.

"I'm sorry, Tom." I tried to make things better. "I didn't know Dirk felt that way."

Tom nodded, and Jacob walked over to him. "He didn't always feel that way, Tom. Just since our pa died. See, he drowned in the harbor while savin' somebody's life. The man he saved was a black man, and Dirk has hated black folks ever since."

"I understand. Too bad a boy so young is full of so much hate. Well, you see this house gettin' built by itself? Will, pick up that board and stretch."

We worked for some time, mostly not talkin'. Nobody knew what to say. We were doing real good on the walls though. Pa was on the ladder, hammerin', when Dirk and Mrs. Caldwell came around from the front of the house. They stopped in front of Pa. "Tell him, Dirk." Mrs. Caldwell was lookin' real stern.

"I'm sorry, sir. I know you ain't my pa, and you know you ain't my pa, but that's no reason for me to say what I did." He was real quiet and kind of stuttering.

"Dirk, you are right. I ain't your pa. I ain't goin' to try to take his place. I am goin' to try to help you grow up to be a respectful man. I won't back away from that. I'm sorry if you don't like that, but I don't know of no other way to help you grow up."

"Yes, sir."

"Now, Tom!" It was Mrs. Caldwell's stern voice again as she stared at Dirk.

I think this was harder for him. "Sorry," he said quiet-like.

Tom nodded at him. "Jacob told us about your daddy. Sounds like you're still pretty mad about it. I lost my daddy when I was about your age, too. He got sold by white men. I hated all white men for a real long time. That hate was turnin' me mean. When I got my freedom, I promised myself I would always hate white folks for what they done to me and my daddy. I was gettin' so mean, I started to hatin' myself. Then I got to thinkin'. It wasn't all white people that did that to me, so why was I hatin' them? Little by little, my hate started to go away. Now, I know this man here and his son, and he says I'm his friend. Can't hate a friend and can't have a friend if'n you don't give people a chance." Dirk just stood there, hangin' his head. "I heard your daddy died savin' a black man. That's no reason to hate. He was savin' a life. You should be proud of him. He was a good man."

Mrs. Caldwell held out her hand and said, "Tom, may I shake your hand?"

"Don't know if that's proper, ma'am."

"It is a proper way to show you my respect."

Tom took her hand real light and real quick. "Thank you, ma'am." He smiled at Dirk and said, "Think we should get these walls up so y'all have a place to live! Dirk, will you hand me the hammer?"

"Yes, sir."

We worked really hard the rest of the day until it was getting dark. Dirk and Jacob went home for supper. We asked Tom to stay with us to eat. "Thank you, but I'll be on my way. I'll take those eggs you promised me and go to the market early to sell them. With all that's goin' on in town, prices are real high."

I got a sack and went into the chicken coop to gather up a few more eggs and then emptied the basket that Pa had in the root cellar. "Here, Tom."

"Can't thank you enough, Tom," said Pa. "Will said you were a good worker. You sure proved it today."

"We can start on the roof tomorrow," was all he said to that, and he was on his way down the path.

• • •

Pa and I talked during supper about what we would do the next day and how long he thought it would take.

"Hopin' to get the roof on tomorrow. We'll be goin' to church to talk to the preacher on Sunday. Then we can make some plans about the rest of it. Got to figure out how much needs to get done before we all move in here and can be comfortable. I think we can get the walls between the rooms done next week, and I'll see how much more Mary wants to have done. I know she wants windows and such, but that can come later."

"You're happy, ain't you, Pa?"

"I am, son. I hope you're happy, too."

"I'm gettin' to be, a little at a time. I was pretty scared about what Dirk said to Tom today, though. After Jacob explained it, I guess I could understand. I don't agree with him, but I understand."

"That's a start, Will. Dirk's a good boy, but he's still hurtin' about his pa. People get over things different. He acts like he's got tough skin, but I think it ain't as tough as he wants it to be."

"How do you suppose Tom knew all that stuff he told Dirk? It ain't like he's had any learnin', but he sure sounded smart."

"Tom's got what I call wisdom. That don't come from books. It comes from livin'—or more than livin'. Some people can go through life and things happen to 'em, and they go on and don't think nothing about what happened, whether it was good or bad. Some people go through life learnin' from what happened to them and take some wisdom from it, especially the bad things. It's easy to hold on to the good things that happen, but it's lots harder to take somethin' good from the bad things and use what you learned to make things better for yourself."

I thought for a minute. "I think I understand. Is that like when Ma died? That was a bad thing. But the good thing we got was Little Sarah."

"Somethin' like that, son. You just keep learnin' from your books, but you got to learn from life and from other people. That's what gives you wisdom. Now I want you to go to bed so's you can get up early to do chores. Tomorrow, you are goin' to school. You ain't been there enough lately, and it's important to keep up."

"But, Pa, we got to work on the house."

"A few hours ain't goin' to make so much difference when we got the extra help. You go and work hard when you get back."

"Yes, sir." I wanted to help him finish the house, but I was glad to be goin'. Didn't know if that would change when we were all one family.

I had just climbed into bed when Pa said, "Will, I have a serious question to ask you." Everything seemed to be real serious lately, so I wasn't surprised. "Will, I'd like you to be my best man."

I got out of bed and stood there, looking at him. "What's that? What do you want me to do?"

He laughed a little, 'cause I guess I sounded a little scared. "It means I would like you to stand up with me at the wedding. It's like you're a part of it. You would hold the ring until the preacher says he wants me to put it on Mary's finger. You would be next to me the whole time."

"Yes, sir. I'd be proud to stand next to you!"

"Thank you, Will. G'night."

I got back into bed and hardly remembered if I put my head down on the pillow.

CHAPTER 18

• • •

I WAS REAL EXCITED TO get to school to tell the Wilsons about Pa and Mrs. Caldwell. They were all sort of surprised to see me. "William, I was afraid that you wouldn't be coming back until after harvest next fall," my teacher said.

"Won't be able to be here much more. There's been lots goin' on."

"Would you like to tell us about it?"

"Yes, ma'am. Pa and Mrs. Caldwell are goin' to get married, and Pa and me been workin' on makin' the cabin into a house because there's goin' to be seven of us livin' there. Little Sarah will be able to live with us, and Mrs. Caldwell's got three boys. Sure will take lots of getting used to."

"My goodness, it certainly will. I'm happy for all of you. I have seen Mary quite often with her boys at church and know her to be a very good person."

"Yes, ma'am. She sure is." I didn't think I should tell about yesterday with Dirk and Tom, but only a nice person would have done what Mrs. Caldwell did.

"When is the wedding?"

"Don't know yet. We'll find out on Sunday when they talk to the preacher."

"I would like it if Mr. Wilson and the children and I could come to the wedding. Do you think that would be all right with your father?"

"Don't know, but I can ask."

"Thank you. And as long as we're talking about changes, Will, I want you to know that we'll only be having school until the end of next week. With the weather warming and fields needing tending, Mr. Wilson says the children must go to work. That was our agreement several years ago. I can teach them for a time in the slow season, but not during growing season."

"Makes sense to me. That'll be good. I won't feel like I'm missin' anything."

"Maybe after the harvest, the other boys and Sarah will want to come with you to school."

"Don't know about that."

"Very well; that's for another time. Now it is time for reading. Here's a newspaper from town. Will, I'd like you to start reading this story about General Beauregard, and then Elizabeth will finish it. We can practice reading and learn what is happening in Charleston at the same time."

I did like the way Mrs. Wilson was always workin' on teachin' us somethin'. Maybe I could learn some of that wisdom Pa was talkin' about from her.

I got to school the next few days but worked double hard when I got home. Tom was there some days to help Pa, and the house was lookin' a lot like it was for a family. I was thinkin' that it could be good to be part of a family again, even if I didn't have Pa all to myself.

After the last day of school, I walked into Charleston to pick up Sarah. Even though she was getting bigger and could walk a lot of the way, I brought the wagon Pa had made for her. The day was warm and muggy, like most days at this time of the year, but when I got near the harbor, there was a cool breeze.

While I was walking through town, I had to walk around a lot of the earthworks and bunkers that were being dug. I got to wonderin' why they were goin' to all that trouble, since Major Anderson would probably run out of supplies soon. I stopped one of the Citadel cadets that was workin' there. "Hey, what's goin' on?"

"Building up defenses against the Yanks. What do you think we're doing?" was his quick answer. Then he turned around. "Oh, it's you. Sorry I sounded so mean, but they been working us pretty hard, trying to get ready."

It took me some time to recognize the cadet. It was Charles Burke. I remembered taking the message about his mother to him when he was workin' on Morris Island. "How's your ma?" I asked before I thought that maybe he didn't want to talk to me about it.

He stopped and took a breath. "She died right after I got home."

"I'm sorry." It seemed like a real weak thing to say when somebody's ma dies, but that was all I could think of.

"Thanks. Sorry, I forgot your name, but I'll never forget what you did for me. It was because of you that I got to her before she passed. She smiled when she saw me." His voice slowed some. "That was her last. I remembered you said your ma died, too. It's really hard. It helped to know that somebody else went through that and was able to keep going."

"Things get better sometimes. My pa is getting married again, and we'll be a family."

"That is happy news. Maybe in a while, I'll start feeling like things are good again, but I don't right now."

"Burke, get to work! You want those damn Yankees walking into town?" someone yelled. The cadet whirled around without another word to me and started hoistin' the logs for a roadblock.

• • •

When I got to the Hawkins' place, I saw somethin' strange. Miss Annie was sittin' on a bench in the garden, her face buried in her hands. Sarah was standin' next to her like she was the grown-up, and she had an arm stretched as far as it could go around Annie's shoulder. "Don't cry, Annie. It's all right. That's what Aunt Fran says. Please don't cry."

Miss Annie looked up at her and gave her a hug. "Sarah, what will I do without you?" She started to cry again.

That was when Sarah saw me. "Tell her, Willie. It's all right."

I said, "I'll try, Sarah. Miss Annie, is there anything I can do to help you?"

"Oh, Will. I wish someone could do something. This is terrible. I know Jeff and the men are running low on supplies, and I see all of the cannons being moved into position to point at the fort. I'm so afraid for him. I feel so helpless, and I'm afraid about what will happen to me. How will I get home?"

"Tell her it will be all right, Willie!" Sarah demanded.

"I hope it will be all right. I'm sure you'll be all right. Mr. Hawkins wouldn't let anything happen to you. Maybe you can go back to New York with him on one of his business trips."

Miss Annie wiped her eyes and smiled a little. "Maybe I can. I will miss you and little Sarah when that happens."

"Annie can't go away!" Sarah was standing with her hands on her hips like we've seen Aunt Fran do when she was giving an order to one of the servants. We both broke out laughing. Sarah could always make us smile.

I turned when I heard the kitchen door open. Aunt Fran called me. "Will! I'd like to talk to you for a minute before you go."

"Sure, Aunt Fran. What is it?"

"I've been thinking about the wedding and trying to figure out what to do for your father and Mary. What do you think about having a little luncheon picnic right at the church after the ceremony?"

"Sounds fine to me."

"I'll need your help then. I would like to know how many people might be there, and I really need to know when the ceremony will be. I don't want to be surprised the day before. Will you tell me as soon as you find out?"

"Sure, Aunt Fran. I'll find out on Sunday, and Sarah and I can come back right after church. That ain't too far for her to walk."

"Thank you, Will. I am so excited for all of you. How do you feel about it?"

"Well, at first I wasn't so sure, but the idea keeps gettin' better in my mind."

"Good. Oh, Will—tell John that Mr. and Mrs. Hawkins would like to be there. They are so fond of Sarah and happy that she will have a proper family."

"I'll tell him. See you on Sunday."

Sarah was quiet for a long way while we were walking home before she asked, "Willie, where is Annie going?"

"She may be going home soon."

"She is home!"

"No, Sarah, she is staying at the Hawkins' just like you do. She is going to school in Charleston, but her home and her family are in New York."

"Can we go visit her?"

"Maybe. It's a long way away. Maybe we could write her a letter after she goes."

"No! I don't know how to write!" Sarah began to sniffle.

"Don't cry. I can write, and I can teach you." A smile returned to her face. She decided that it was time to share the wagon with Dolly.

In my head, I thanked Ma for teaching me things and making me want to learn. Even if I didn't get to all the places I was reading about, I could help my sister. Ma would have been happy about that. I wondered if Ma would have been happy about Pa gettin' married again. She probably would, because she'd know that we would be a family again.

Pa was waitin' for us when we got back. "Thought you'd be back a little sooner than this," he said, lookin' at me.

"Well, sir, part of it is 'cause I had some slowin' down in town. They're buildin' all kinds of barriers and roadblocks. Guess they're afraid the Yankees will get into Charleston. Don't know how they think that, 'cause Miss Annie says they'll run out of food and they're waitin' for orders to go back to New York."

"Pa, Annie is going away to New York. I don't want her to go!"

"I know, Sarah." Pa got down on his knees so he could look her in her eyes. "Sometimes people don't always do what we want them to, but they do what they have to do. I'm sure she doesn't want to leave, but it is best if she's at her home, just like you will be at your home very soon. Do you like it?" Pa pointed at the house. "Come in and see your new room. It is real close to Mary and me."

She skipped into the house and looked around. "It's got real big, Pa!"

"Yes, so we can all be together all the time."

"Is there a room for Annie and Aunt Fran?"

Pa paused. "No, but we will see Aunt Fran a lot of times."

"What about Mr. and Mrs. Hawkins? Do they have a room?"

Pa paused again, "Well…" he started.

"Pa," I interrupted, "That reminds me. Mr. and Mrs. Hawkins want to come to the wedding. Aunt Fran told me. I think that's special that rich people like them want to come, don't you?"

"Well, that is a surprise. I s'pose if they want to, then they're welcome. They're probably thinkin' about Sarah. I know they'll miss her. I'll talk to

Mary on Sunday. We sure aren't plannin' on makin' it big. Just thought it would be a quiet thing."

"Aunt Fran said I should let her know Sunday after church when it will be, so she can have a picnic lunch ready for after. Oh, and the Wilsons want to be there, too."

"Didn't think so many people cared. Well, Mary and me got some serious talkin' to do on Sunday about the weddin' and about what to do with her place. I know she really doesn't want to sell it, but we can't keep up two farms."

I had been thinkin' some on the way home. "Pa, I have an idea that might work." He looked at me. "Well…" I kind of stuttered because it was a real strange idea. "Well, what if Tom lived there?"

"Tom? Why should we let Tom live there?"

"I don't mean just live there. What if he worked the farm and gave you and Mrs. Caldwell part of what he grows? He'd have a place to live, she could keep her farm, and there would be extra comin' in."

"Hmmm. I'll have to think on that and talk to Mary. I guess if it didn't work out, we could always sell the land then. Where'd you come up with an idea like that?"

"Don't know, Pa. Just seemed like it could work for everybody. Since their fields are all planted, it might not be too big of a job for him."

"Hmmm."

By this time, Sarah was getting restless, so we went fishin' for dinner.

• • •

Sunday morning, we had a full wagon going to church. The Caldwells walked over early, and Mrs. Caldwell brought fresh corn muffins. I went to the root cellar to get the butter Pa had made me churn the day before. It had taken twice as long because Sarah wanted to do it too, but it was worth it. Pa made a pot of coffee and decided we had time for a little more breakfast before church.

On the way, Rhett kept Sarah gigglin' while Pa and Mrs. Caldwell talked quiet in the seat. Me and the boys were in the back, makin' some plans of our own for where we could go huntin', and maybe with the three of us, we could go out for more than a day and spend the night under the stars upriver.

We got to church and had to hurry in just as it was startin'. The church was full. By this time in April, most plantin' is done, so folks have some time for church. Lots of them come to see friends and get news about what's happened since the last time they were there. The Wilsons were there, and Mrs. Wilson and Mrs. Caldwell smiled at each other. Then we all paid attention to the pastor—all of us 'cept Sarah, who was squirmin' around until I told her that if Dolly could sit quiet, so could she.

After we sang the hymns and heard how God loved us and how we had to do good things to help people, Pastor Riley said the last "amen," and we could get up and move. Mrs. Wilson came over to talk to Mrs. Caldwell, and Pa followed the pastor out the door to talk to him. The five of us decided we could go out too and maybe play a game of tag while the grown-ups got things figured out. It didn't take long for all of the Wilsons to join in the game.

By the time Pa and Mrs. Caldwell were done talking to the pastor, our game got real small. The Wilsons left first—I supposed right after they knew what day the wedding would be. By then, Sarah was getting tired of trying to catch somebody, Dirk got bored, and Rhett went to his ma to see what was going on.

Pa walked over to us. He smiled, picked up Sarah, and gave her a hug. "Well, young lady, you will have a new mother in four days. Pastor Riley says Thursday at eleven o'clock is the best time for him, so Thursday, April eleventh, it is."

"I'll tell Aunt Fran. Are the Wilsons going to be here? What should I tell her about the Hawkins?" I asked.

"Mr. and Mrs. Wilson will be. I don't think the young ones care, so they probably won't. As far as the Hawkins, they can come if they'd like. Now, Sarah, Will is goin' to take you back to Aunt Fran for a few more days so we can all get ready for Thursday."

"I want to stay with my ma and you and Willie!"

"Not right now," Pa said quietly. "But soon."

I said, "Come on, Sarah, I'll race you to see Miss Annie." She hung her head, but she followed me. "In only four days, we'll all be together," I told her as we walked toward Meeting Street. "Do you know how long that will be? You only go to sleep at Aunt Fran's this many more nights." I held up four fingers "Then Pa and Mrs. Caldwell will be married."

"Do I have to call her Mrs. Caldwell? I thought she would be my ma."

"She will, in this many days," and I held up my fingers again.

"All right," she sighed. Then she saw Miss Annie. "Annie! I know about my ma. It will be in this many days." She held up four fingers and ran to get a hug. I went into the house to tell Aunt Fran about the wedding.

CHAPTER 19

• • •

WE ONLY HAD A FEW days to get a lot of things finished in the house. We couldn't do it all by then, but it sure wasn't a cabin anymore. Pa wanted to finish a big table so we could all sit and eat together right away. I was workin' on one of the benches when Pa asked, "You all right with this now, Will?"

"I think so, Pa. I know you and Sarah are goin' to be real happy, and I like Mrs. Caldwell a lot and I like her boys. I'm just trying to work out how different it'll all be."

"You're right about that. But I want you to be happy, too."

"Is it good enough to work into bein' happy?" I asked him after a minute.

"You know, Will, that's a good question, and I'd say that the smartest thing to do is to work into it. This ain't somethin' you can just turn on like a lamp. Keep in mind, this is goin' to take time for all of us, but I believe it is the best thing we can do. And you need to start thinkin' about what you are goin' to call Mary. You can't call her Mrs. Caldwell after the wedding, and I don't think it would be right to call her Mrs. McShane. Do you?" He laughed a little, but I knew he was right.

I went back to finishing the bench, but I couldn't help thinkin' and blurted out, "Pa, the thing that I'm most scared of is havin' to share you."

He stopped hammerin' and looked me square in the eye. "Will, you ain't never goin' to share my love with nobody. You might have to share my time, but never my love." He paused. "Funny thing about love. You never have to divide it. It only multiplies." He could always make me feel better. I was happier already.

Just then Tom showed up. "Was meanin' to get here earlier, Mr. John. Had trouble gettin' through town. They's so much goin's-on there, what with roadblocks and soldiers and the like. One of 'em thought I was a slave and told me to get to work, and it took some time to set that all straight so's I could get here."

"That's fine, Tom. Any help you can give us is appreciated. I am glad you're here, though. I have somethin' important to talk to you about." Tom looked a little nervous. "No, Tom. It's nothin' bad. I think it's pretty good, and you might, too. Let me see if I can explain this in the right way." Pa paused. Tom was quiet. "You know Mrs. Caldwell and I are gettin' married on Thursday."

"Yes, sir. Sure would like to be there to see it."

"Certainly, Tom. I didn't know that, but we'd like you to come."

"Eleven o'clock at the church on the way into town!" I blurted out.

"That's settled. Now, I got a question for you. Mrs. Caldwell and I don't want to sell her place right now. Things are all mixed up, what with the talk of war and all the goin's-on in the city. We'd like to keep the land, but we would need somebody to take care of it for us. Live in the cabin, tend the crops, and harvest what we've already got planted. I know it would be a lot of work, but we wondered if you would be interested in doin' that for us." Tom didn't say anything but looked like he was thinkin'. "You wouldn't have to do all the work. We've got four boys that could help out sometimes."

Tom stroked his chin. "Hmmm."

"In return for your work, you would have a place to live, food from the garden, and get a share of the crop. We think twenty percent would be fair."

"Hmmm. Gots to think on it for a minute." There was a long pause. "I got a brother, Moses. Would he be able to live there and work with me? We could probably take care of the place ourselves."

"I don't know why not. Then you and your brother would have a place, and we could keep the land at least for another year until all this ruckus about the Yankees is over."

"Hmmm. Don't know 'bout twenty p'cent. Don't know what that means."

"Well," Pa started to explain, "That's part of the crop you could keep, and we would get eighty percent."

"Don't know what that means, neither."

I had to smile. Just because Tom didn't have proper education didn't make him stupid. I could tell he was tryin' to work a deal with Pa. I interrupted. "Tom, twenty percent is like if you harvest five bales of cotton for us, you would get to keep one, and we would get four."

"Hmmm. So me and Moses could live there and eat outta the garden and take care of the place and harvest your crop, and we'd get one bale for every five?"

"That's right," said Pa.

"Hmmm." He paused again. "Two bales and I'll talk to Moses."

"Two?"

"Yes, sir. Way I figure, we'd be doin' you and the missus a big favor by tendin' your land. So you make it two bales and I'll talk to Moses. I could tell you right soon what he says, but it sounds good to me."

Pa smiled. "Two it is." He held out his hand. Tom took it and shook hard. I think he was proud of himself for helpin' his brother and us and himself.

"Let's get this table finished!"

• • •

On Wednesday, we took the wagon to the Caldwells' to load up some of the furniture from their place. With the wedding the next day, they wanted to have as much of our new home ready as they could. "How is it looking, John?" Mrs. Caldwell asked.

"Gettin' close. We'll go back and finish the bunk beds for the boys and pick up the feather beds tomorrow. Don't really want to do that on our weddin' day, but can't think of any other time."

"I understand, John. It has to be done."

"Mr. McShane, Will and Jacob and I can do that," Dirk offered.

"Thank you Dirk. I suppose you can. Do you think that maybe you could call me somethin' besides Mr. McShane?"

"I'll have to think on that, sir. I don't mean no offense, but callin' you 'Pa' just don't seem right."

"I take no offense, Dirk. That will be one more thing we can work out in time. We will have lots of it." Pa put his arm around Dirk's shoulder. I couldn't tell if Pa pulled him a little closer or if Dirk moved that way on his own. I think he was right again about love multiplying.

"Come on, boys. Help me with this chair."

"Are you ready for this, Will?" Mrs. Caldwell asked me when they were out at the wagon.

"Yes, ma'am. My good shirt is clean, and I even have shoes to wear to church. Not too sure my feet'll be happy in shoes this time of the year, but Pa says I have to."

"My boys, too. But I didn't mean your clothes. I mean are *you* ready?" She said the word "you" louder than the rest.

"I think so, ma'am. Guess it'll take some gettin' used to. Pa says things don't have to stay the same to be good."

"Your pa is a good man, and he's right. We know this will be hardest on you boys. Take all the time you need."

"Yes, ma'am."

"And Will, I hope you won't call me Mrs. Caldwell anymore."

"No, ma'am, but…"

"I know," she interrupted me. "Ma don't seem right, at least now. You could call me Mary."

"I don't think Pa would like that."

"How about if we start with Miss Mary and see what happens?"

"Yes, ma'am." That would be one more thing I would need to work into.

• • •

I'd never seen Pa like he was the next mornin'. He was as nervous as a cat on a porcupine. He started breakfast and then went off to get dressed, but he came out of his room with no shirt and got more eggs to break into the frying pan.

"Pa, you already put six in there. I'll make breakfast. You go shave and get dressed so as we can get to the church."

"Get to the church. Right." Off he went again, and I took over the frying pan.

When the eggs were done, I took the pan off the stove and heard some terrible mooin'. I called out, "Pa, be right back! We been so flustered this mornin', we forgot to milk the cows." We had two now 'cause we brought the Caldwells' back with us yesterday.

By the time I got back in, Pa was sitting at the big, new table with an empty plate in front of him. I don't think I'd ever seen him look so good. His face was shaved clean, his hair was combed proper, and his tie was in a neat bow. "You look good, Pa. Do you want some eggs?"

He looked at his plate and laughed. "Glad you're here to take care of me, son. Guess I'm more nervous than I thought I'd be."

"Seems so." I laughed with him.

• • •

Pa asked me four times if I had the ring on the way to church. I finally pulled it out of my pocket to show him. I told him I was hangin' on to it and wouldn't lose it. He took a deep breath and relaxed a little the rest of the way there. When we got to the church, Pa wiped his hand on his pants before he shook hands with the pastor.

It wasn't long before Aunt Fran came in a carriage with Sarah and Miss Annie. They pulled out baskets of azaleas that were blooming all over this time of year. We carried them into the church, where they brightened it with splashes of white, pink, and red.

"Papa, look at my new dress! See the flowers on my bonnet."

"It isn't exactly a new dress," said Annie. "Just some new lace on it, and fresh flowers in the bonnet you gave her for her birthday."

"You look lovely, Sarah," said Aunt Fran.

She beamed like she was the bride. "Thank you, Auntie."

"Here they come," said Miss Annie quietly. "Sarah, do you remember what I told you?"

Sarah smiled again. "Sit quiet and look pretty!"

"Yes. When we're in church, sit quietly so you look pretty." I wondered if that would work, but I didn't think Pa would be too upset if it didn't.

"Huh." Pa had turned toward the road. He caught his breath when he saw the Caldwells' wagon. Dirk was drivin', and his mother was sitting next to him. I knew why Pa reacted like that. She looked beautiful. She was pretty, but today she was really somethin' special. The dress she was wearin' was light green with flowers all over, and her hair was like curls that were fallin' out from under a light green veil. I was proud of her and proud she would be my mother, too.

Pa sort of stuttered, "Mary, you look beautiful."

"Thank you, John," she said and sort of blushed. "Will you please help me down from the wagon?" I think Pa forgot she needed to get down. He hurried over and took her hand. Dirk smiled.

The Wilsons and the Hawkins were there a few minutes later, and Pastor Riley said it was time for us to all go into church. I looked around but didn't see Tom. I guessed he changed his mind. Everybody sat down on the benches except Pa, Mrs. Caldwell, and me. We went to the front and stood while the pastor read from the Bible and said some nice things about Pa and my new ma. He talked to each of them, and they answered him, and he asked if there was a ring. Pa looked at me. I smiled and took it out of my pocket and gave it to him to put on her finger. Then the pastor said, "I now pronounce you man and wife. You may kiss the bride."

Pa hesitated and gave Mrs. Caldwell—I had to start thinking of her as Miss Mary—a quick kiss, and Sarah jumped up. "Are you my mother now?"

"Yes, Sarah, I am. I have never had a little girl before, so I hope I'm a good mother to you."

Hands on hips, Sarah replied, "I'm a big girl!"

"Of course you are, dear," Miss Mary stuttered. "You are just littler than the boys."

"Oh." Sarah seemed satisfied with that and gave her a hug.

"Everyone, please join us for a wonderful picnic that Fran and Annie have made for us to celebrate. Boys, will you help them with the baskets?"

As we went out, the Hawkins were walkin' up to Pa and Miss Mary, and I saw Mr. Hawkins shake Pa's hand. They talked while we set out the blankets in the churchyard, and the fried chicken and biscuits and pies. They smiled and waved as they walked past us, and Aunt Fran explained that they couldn't stay because of a meeting Mr. Hawkins had in Columbia. He needed to catch the train.

Just then, I saw Tom walkin' away. "Tom, I was afraid you weren't comin'. Where are you goin'?"

"Oh, I sure wouldn't miss this. Y'all look so good and so happy. I think it's time for me to leave now. Wouldn't be proper for me to stay."

"Of course it would, Tom." Miss Mary was walkin' toward us. "We would be honored to have you as our guest at the picnic. Please stay." Pa was noddin' at him, too.

"Don't seem quite right, but if'n you want me to, I will." Even though he was a freedman, I guess he still thought like a slave.

We ate and laughed, and Pa told stories about when I was a baby and I fell into the river and almost drowned. When he pulled me out, I tried to go back in and do it again. Miss Mary smiled and said, "We both have a lot to learn about all of our children."

The Wilsons left right after we finished eatin', sayin' they had to get back so everyone could finish their chores. Mr. Wilson shook Pa's hand, and Mrs. Wilson hugged Miss Mary.

Aunt Fran and Miss Annie were packing up the baskets when Pa said, "Fran, this was real nice. Mary and I thank you and Miss Annie for making this a little more special."

"It was our pleasure, wasn't it, Annie?"

"It certainly was. I was very happy to be a part of it. I will miss all of you whenever I do go back to New York. I think it may be sooner rather than later. I'm still uncertain, but I will continue to believe that Jefferson will be able to arrange travel."

"We hope you will be all right and find some way to get back home. I can't thank you enough for all that you've done for Sarah. I know she will be real sad when you go." Pa looked over to where Sarah was playing with Rhett.

"I'm happy you all have a family again. I hope that you live like the fairy tale that Sarah likes so much—happily ever after." Miss Mary smiled and thanked her.

We heard Aunt Fran's stern voice. "Now, John and Mary, there is one more thing that will be your wedding present from me. I would like the children to come home with me for a few days so you two can get that house in order. It will be a lot easier without the young ones there."

"That's too much, Fran," said Pa, and Miss Mary looked a little red.

"No discussion! All of us will get a chance to get to know each other a little better. I won't be seeing Will and Sarah so much now, and I don't know the other boys at all. I'd like us to get acquainted. The Hawkins will be in Columbia for a while, so the house will be quiet. Why don't you come and pick them up Saturday afternoon? You can stay for dinner, and then the whole family can go home together." Aunt Fran said it all so fast that Pa didn't have time to interrupt.

He looked at Fran and then Miss Mary. His new wife nodded a little, and he said, "You win again, Fran. How can I argue with two women?"

Aunt Fran took charge. "Boys, tuck the baskets in tight so we can all fit. You will all be coming home with me until Saturday."

Rhett looked scared. "Ma, should I go too?"

Miss Mary didn't have time to respond when Aunt Fran said, "Certainly, Rhett. I'll need your help to keep Sarah entertained, especially if Annie must leave us."

"Boys, it will be a great help to me and John if you stay with Fran. It's only for two days, and we'll get everything ready for you at home."

"But, Ma, I can help!" Rhett was sort of whinin'.

"Don't be such a baby, Rhett." I could tell Dirk would be happy to stay in Charleston for two days and didn't want Rhett to ruin his chance.

"Dirk, stop that." Miss Mary was real firm.

"Yes, ma'am."

"Jacob, is that all right with you?"

"Sure. It'll be fun, Rhett. There's lots to see in Charleston."

"That's right." Pa got into the conversation, not sounding so sure about the plan now. "What if somethin' happens, Fran? I know there's been a lot of talk about Fort Sumter and all."

"What can happen, John? The Confederate Army, the South Carolina militia, and the cadets from the Citadel are all around us to protect us from eighty-five starving men three miles out in the harbor."

"I suppose you're right. It's fine with me, then. We'll pick them up on Saturday."

We finished packin' up the buggy. Dirk and I said we could walk. It wasn't that far. Jacob decided to walk with us, and we were on our way to Charleston.

• • •

THE BUGGY WAS WAY AHEAD of us, so Dirk must have felt safe about talkin', because he said, "This is goin' to be somethin'. Ain't never been to Charleston without Ma watchin' every move."

"Well, we still have Aunt Fran. She keeps a close eye on me when I'm there. Always wants to know where I'm goin' and makin' sure I stay away from some places. It ain't all that excitin', especially now with all the soldiers and bunkers and cannons set around everywhere."

"That's what I want to find out about. I think I should be in there helpin', 'cept for this damn arm!"

"Dirk!" Jacob yelled. "You know Ma don't like no swearin'!"

"Ya see, Will? Somebody's always watchin'. If not Ma, then one of the two little baby boys that're my brothers. They're really mama's boys!" Dirk made a face at Jacob and punched his arm.

I wasn't sure what I should do or if I should do anything, so I said, "Well, I guess we're all kind of brothers now, and we should be lookin' out after each other. If Pa and your ma didn't think we would do that, they probably wouldn't let us stay with Aunt Fran. No matter what, we can't be givin' her a bad time. She's been almost like a ma to me and Sarah for a long time."

After a pause, Dirk nodded and said, "Guess you're right. Don't mean to give nobody a bad time, but I ain't a baby anymore. There's things I want to do. This bum arm has stopped me from doin' a lot of them."

I couldn't blame him for bein' sort of bitter about his arm. He was a little older than me, but his father had been gone for a while, and he had been the man of the house for his ma and brothers since. He didn't want to feel like he was goin' backwards about growin' up, especially now. There were boys probably younger than him helpin' the soldiers and talkin' about beatin' the Yankees. I was pretty sure he wanted to be part of it.

We had to take a longer way than usual, not just because of all the barriers and cannons pointed every which way, but because of all the people in the street. When we stopped in front of the Hawkins', I asked Aunt Fran what was goin' on. Miss Annie started to cry. Aunt Fran told us, "General Beauregard has been sending messages to Fort Sumter, telling them they must evacuate. Major Anderson has been sending messages back, telling him they weren't going to. Annie is extremely upset because she can't get word from her brother about what she should do, and, of course, she is extremely worried about him."

"With all that happenin', I'm surprised Pa let us come."

"Your father doesn't know, Will. I kept it from him on purpose. Whatever happens here should not ruin their wedding day and the few days they have alone together. They need to spend some time getting to know each other without a gaggle of youngsters around."

Just then, Terrance ran up to the carriage to help unload but also to share the news. "The genr'l says they gots to go, or they's goin' be shot at with all them cannons!"

Miss Annie began to wail, "No! They can't do that."

"Yes'm, they can, and everybody's getting ready fer it!"

Dirk got a big smile on his face, Jacob's eyes got real big, and Rhett turned white and started to cry. Sarah put her arm around him and said, "Everything will be all right, Rhett. Won't it, Auntie Fran?"

"Of course it will. None of you need worry. I would have not brought you here if I thought there would be danger. Remember, there have been threats about attacks for months, and nothing has happened. There's no reason to think this time will be different."

"Yes'm, it's different. This time, they's boats with Yankee supplies comin', and I hear by the battery them soldiers ain't lettin' those boats in. And they'll blow the fort back to New York if'n they have to." Miss Annie cried louder.

"That's enough, Terrance. Take those baskets into the house. And we don't want to hear any more rumors!" Aunt Fran sounded stern.

"Ain't no rumor, Miss Fran. It be true!"

"Terrance, go now!"

"Yes'm." He filled his arms and disappeared into the house.

"Don't fret, Annie." Aunt Fran had her arm around Miss Annie now.

Sarah decided she needed to help Annie, too. "It will be all right," she said as she moved from Rhett's side and took Miss Annie's hand. "Don't cry. Auntie Fran can make it all right."

Miss Annie stopped sobbin' and tried to smile at Sarah. "Yes, Sarah. I'm sure she will."

"Annie, you will start by getting all of your things together and ready yourself to go. I don't think there will be a great hurry, but it will be good to be ready, and I believe you will feel better if you do. Sarah, I need you and Rhett to help me take the rest of the things into the kitchen. Rhett, if it will make you more comfortable, you may stay inside with Sarah and me. You three boys take the carriage around to the stable. Will, then show the boys where you will sleep, and lay out blankets. We won't let all of this spoil our day. We may have to stay close to home, but we still can be out in the garden. If anything does happen, we have a good view."

"Yes, ma'am." I think we all said it at the same time.

After we had things put away, Aunt Fran thought we could all use another piece of chocolate cake. While we were in the kitchen, Dirk asked if it would be all right for us to go across to the park, which was very near the battery.

Aunt Fran hesitated for a minute. She said, "I suppose you boys are old enough to go and smart enough not to get into any trouble. Can I trust you? Your pa would never forgive me if anything happened to you."

"You know you can, Aunt Fran," I said.

"Dirk? Would your mother let you go?"

"No!" interrupted Rhett.

"You keep out of this, baby!" Dirk turned to Aunt Fran. "I really don't know, ma'am, but Will and I talked on the way over. I ain't goin' to be givin' you a hard time. That's a promise."

"Dirk, how about if you call me Aunt Fran, too. It sounds more like family, and that's what we are now. Jacob, are you going to go with them?"

He finished the piece of cake in his mouth real slow. "Maybe I should stay here just in case Rhett gets scared again."

"That's a good idea, Jacob," said Aunt Fran. Then she lowered her voice. "Boys, I'd like you to keep your ears open and listen to what is going on. You may hear more news, though I hope there are no more rumors that aren't true. I'm not worried about us. We are very safe here, but I'd like to know more, if we can, to help Annie figure out what to do. Be back by dark, no matter what. We'll have a light supper tonight, and I will want you to be here."

"We'll do that, Aunt Fran," Dirk said before I had a chance to say anything. It was somethin' else I'd need to get used to. We finished the cake and headed across the street.

● ● ●

"As many times as I've been here lately and as many folks as I've seen 'round the battery, I ain't never seen it like this," I told Dirk. "Looks like somethin' special is goin' on. Hey." I tapped on the shoulder of a man in a nice coat and hat. "What's happenin'?"

"You haven't heard? General Beauregard sent that Yankee Anderson an order to leave today or he'd attack Fort Sumter. Looks like everybody here is hoping that will happen so we can send those damn Yankees back home with their tails between their legs!"

"But why now? They been at the fort for months."

"Where have you been, boy? The slave-loving Lincoln is sending supplies to the fort. Guess President Davis won't let that happen. This is a free country, and sending in supplies and reinforcements is the same as invading. We are sending a loud and clear message to Lincoln—get his troops off of our soil! That's why cannons been firing around here the last two days. Aiming them and getting the range adjusted."

"Wow! Cannons! That is excitin'! Glad we're here, Will. I don't want to miss this!"

"Poor Miss Annie. She's real scared for her brother," I said.

"If they're Yankees, they deserve it," returned Dirk.

"That's true," said the man. "We need to show them they are not wanted here and we will protect our country! When we get them out of here, we can get back to normal!" He walked away into the crowd, wavin' at somebody near one of the cannons.

"Never thought there would be so much excitement here."

"It is excitin', but it's sort of scary, thinkin' that people will be shootin' at each other."

"Will, how else do we get rid of 'em? I ain't been here as much as you, but I know that Beauregard asked them to leave a long time ago, and they wouldn't go. Time we stood up to them cowards hidin' in that fort!"

"Maybe they will just leave so it's all quiet again." Guess I said that to myself more than to Dirk, rememberin' how nice it used to be to come here when everybody wasn't all riled up. "I think we should go back and let Aunt Fran know what we found out."

"You go ahead if you want. I'm waitin' around here to see what happens."

"I'll wait a while, too." I didn't want to leave Dirk by himself. I sort of felt responsible for him even though he was older than me.

We walked through the crowd and listened to more folks talkin'. Some were sayin' that they'd start shellin' the fort any minute. Others thought it wouldn't happen until tomorrow. Some were afraid the supply ships would get to the fort first. Some thought they saw a big ship with cannons pointin' at Charleston. Didn't know who to believe. It was startin' to get dark, so we did have to get back.

We told Aunt Fran and Miss Annie everything we'd heard. Miss Annie cried a little, Jacob's eyes got real big again, and Rhett hung on to Aunt Fran's apron. She said, "All of you listen to me. There won't be any cannons. Even if there are, we are all safe. General Beauregard and all the troops will see to that, so everyone can relax. Annie, see that you are ready to go and also remember that you have a safe place to stay as long as you need it."

"Auntie Fran...everything will be all right, won't it?"

"Yes, Sarah. The rest of you remember that, too. Now, let's have supper and get your beds ready for tonight. Don't forget that you are here so that

John and Mary can have some time alone before they have five children to take care of. We will not let this spoil their time, will we?" She mostly looked at Rhett, who shook his head, even though I could tell he wanted his mother. "If anything happens during the night, you can find out all about it in the morning."

"Seems like it's pretty loud out there, Aunt Fran. Do you really think we'll be able to sleep with all those folks in the park? They look like they're ready to spend the night. They got blankets and picnics like it's a holiday."

"We'll just have to do our best, Dirk. We won't be able to change anything, so we will just go on like it's a regular day. Who will help me get the table ready for dinner?"

I volunteered, 'cause I wasn't sure if anybody else would. I'm still learnin' about the other boys. Jacob and Rhett helped some, but Dirk stood at the window, lookin' out at the park and the battery. I think he was hopin' somethin' would happen. I was sure hopin' it wouldn't. I would have liked for all this talk about war and attacks to stop so we could get on with our life. That, all by itself, would be hard enough.

When everything was ready, Miss Annie came in holding Sarah's hand. She took a deep breath and said, "I'm as ready as I can be until I find out what is going to happen. I think Sarah is hungry, but I doubt that I could eat a bite."

"Please try to eat a little, Annie." Aunt Fran sounded like she was askin' for a favor. "It won't help anybody if you get weak and sick. Now, let's all sit down."

• • •

After supper, Aunt Fran got out extra blankets and pillows and sent us up to one of the empty servant rooms on the third floor of the house. "I'm sure you will all be able to make beds that are comfortable enough for two nights."

When we got upstairs, the other three just sort of looked around. Rhett's eyes were real big now, and he asked, "Do you always get to sleep way up here whenever you want to, Will?"

"No. I don't stay here very often. When I do, I usually sleep downstairs and stay out of the way. With four of us, I guess this is as out of the way as we can get."

"Look out that window, Dirk. We can see the battery and way out into the harbor."

Dirk went over to the window that Jacob was staring out of. "This is a good spot to be," said Dirk. "When somethin' starts, we'll be able to see it from here. I don't think I'll be sleepin' at all."

Rhett's lip was quiverin' a little. "What can start, Dirk?"

"Don't be a baby, Rhett. A war can start and we will be right here when it does!"

Rhett started to cry, but Jacob put his arm around his little brother. "Oh, Rhett. You know Dirk is just teasin' you like he always does." He gave Dirk a dirty look and added, "Remember what Ma told you."

"Jacob is right. I was just teasin' you, Rhett. Nothin' will happen."

I figured we needed to change the talk. "How 'bout we make up those beds?" It didn't take long and it was too early to go to bed, so we decided to see if Aunt Fran would let us go out into the courtyard.

She said she thought it would be all right for a little while, but we could not go one step farther and must come in when she called us. We agreed and the other three went out to look around. I stopped at the door and turned around.

"Aunt Fran, can I ask you a question?"

"Certainly, Will. What is it?"

"It's about the ring. You gave it to Pa for Miss Mary, but he said you were supposed to have it. Why didn't you keep it?"

She sat down and pointed at the chair next to her for me to sit. "Many years ago "I was going to marry a wonderful man named Cyrus. He had just graduated from the Citadel. We were very happy and all ready to make plans for the wedding and start our new life together.

"Your father's and my pa had died a year or so earlier, and at that time, our mother took off the ring she had worn since they were married. She said it was a sad reminder every time she looked at her hand. She told me it would make her proud if I wore it when I was married. She knew it would have made our pa proud, too. So that's how I came to get the ring."

"But what about Cyrus and the wedding?"

"That was the hardest part. It was just when the war with Mexico started. Cyrus had to go to defend our country. I never saw him again."

"Is that why you never got married?"

"Yes, Will. I never found another that I felt I could be happy with, and I was always afraid something could happen again. All I had left was the letter telling me that Cyrus died bravely in a battle that his regiment had finally won. Do you know what the strangest thing is?"

I shook my head.

"The letter was signed by Captain Robert Anderson."

CHAPTER 21

• • •

AUNT FRAN LET ME SHOW the boys around some of the house. We could only look into the parlor and the dining room, but we could visit the ballroom and the library. "This is my favorite place in the whole, big house," I told them in the library. "Mr. Hawkins lets me look at his books and has even let me borrow some of them. He's real nice."

"Why would you want to borrow books?" asked Dirk. "Ain't you got better things to do? I'd rather be huntin' and fishin'."

"I like huntin' and fishin' too, but books can tell you about people and places you can't go to."

"If you can't go there, why do you need to know about 'em?"

"It gives you new ideas and ways to think to about things so you can try to make them better."

"Only way to make things better is to get rid of those damn Yankees!"

"I'm tellin' Ma, Dirk!"

"Go ahead, baby Rhett. See if I care. In two more years when I'm sixteen, I can do whatever I want!"

"You ain't sixteen yet," Jacob said under his breath. Dirk stormed out of the room. I watched him go and must have looked surprised because Jacob said, "Don't mind him, Will. Every now and again, he gets ornery like that, mostly since Pa died. I think he's hurtin' about it more now that Ma and Mr. McShane...oops"—he caught himself—"now that Ma and Mr. John are married. He used to be real gentle."

"I can understand, because sometimes I feel that way when I think about my ma. Sure hope he gets used to my pa, though. He's really a good man. How about we go upstairs and try to get some sleep and hope nothin' happens tonight?"

Rhett seemed to want to stay close to Aunt Fran. I took his hand and said we could go upstairs and pretend we were on an adventure. That seemed to help him a little. He finally asked, "What kind of adventure, Will?"

"Should we pretend we are out exploring all of the land out in the West?" We had learned a little bit about Lewis and Clark in school last week. "We've been out exploring and mapping and finding all sorts of new animals, and we have to go to our cabin and write it all down and sleep so we can go explore again tomorrow."

"What kind of animals?"

He was sure makin' it harder for me. "I don't know. What kind would you like to find?" He started talkin' about furry animals with funny colors as we went upstairs. I looked back at Aunt Fran and nodded a sort of "Good night." She smiled and nodded back.

Dirk was at the window when we got up there. "Look at all them people on the battery. Wish we could be out there."

"Me, too." I only wanted to be there a little. I felt a lot safer in the house.

"Do you think Aunt Fran would let us go out early tomorrow if we didn't bother her again tonight?"

"Maybe. Guess that depends on what's happenin'."

"I'm goin' to bed now so I can get up early. I don't want to miss anything."

"Good idea for all of us," I said.

Dirk chose the spot near the window alongside Jacob. Rhett and I were on the other side of the room. Didn't take long before I heard what sounded like somebody breathin' easy in their sleep and then a little bit of snifflin' from Rhett. "Will," he whispered. "You sleepin'?"

"No. What's wrong?"

"I don't ever think I been away a night from Ma. Do you think she's all right?"

"Sure she is. She's with Pa. They're workin' on the house so's we can all live there in a couple of days. Don't worry."

"Will," he whispered a little later. "I'm scared."

"No need to be scared, Rhett. We're right here, and Aunt Fran is downstairs, and we're safe inside."

"Do you think I'm a baby, Will? Dirk thinks I'm a baby."

"No, Rhett. You ain't a baby. You're a boy who lost his pa, and I think that makes you feel scared sometimes. You ain't a baby."

"I'm goin' like havin' you for a big brother, Will."

"Go to sleep." He was quiet and started breathin' easy.

• • •

I drifted off to sleep but woke up with a start. Then I heard it again. It was cannons in the distance. I'd heard them before, but never this many in a row, and never in the middle of the night. Louder than the cannons, though, was all the cheerin' comin' from the battery across the street. I can't remember hearin' so many people bein' so loud. Dirk was at the window fast as he could get out of bed. Jacob was rubbin' his eyes, and Rhett was startin' to whimper. "I want to be out there," said Dirk. "I don't suppose Aunt Fran would mind. All those people think it's worth seein', and so do I. It must be close to morning anyway. She won't care, will she?"

"I don't know, Dirk. We can go ask her. I don't guess she'd be sleepin' through all the noise anyhow."

The four of us went down to the kitchen, with Rhett holdin' on to my hand. There was a lamp lit on the table, but the room was empty. We went to knock on Aunt Fran's door, but it was open, and she wasn't in there. We finally found her sitting on the front porch, holdin' Sarah in her lap and trying to calm Miss Annie, who was cryin' pretty hard. "I was wondering how long it would take you boys," she said to us. "I suppose you want to go out and join the crowd."

"Yes, ma'am," answered Dirk.

"I think it will be all right. Rhett, would you like to stay here with Annie and me?" He shook his head and let go of my hand. He got real close to Aunt Fran until Miss Annie said that he could sit on her lap. It didn't take but a minute before he snuggled into the chair with her. "Jacob," Aunt Fran said, "how about you staying here with us? I think it would help Rhett and Sarah."

"Yes, ma'am." His voice sounded real relieved. He was more scared than I thought.

"You two may go and join the crowd. Stay out of trouble. Lots of those folks started celebrating and drinking yesterday, so they can get ornery. Come on home when it gets light and you want some breakfast." I asked what time it was. "Four thirty," she answered. "Seems like a fool time to start a fight!"

We both agreed but were across the street in no time. She was right about people celebratin'. They were whoopin' and dancin' and singin' songs about sendin' Yankees back to Lincoln. It was easy to get caught up in it all.

When we pushed close to the cannons on the battery, I saw Charles Burke in his Citadel uniform, lookin' pretty important. He saw me at the same time and nodded. "You plan on firin' that cannon?" I asked.

"I would if I had to, but the fort is too far away. I have to be here instead of out there. Wish I could have been at Fort Johnson when they started firing this morning."

I looked at Dirk and forgot he hadn't met Charles. I introduced them real quick and told Dirk about goin' out to Morris Island to deliver a message to Charles from his father. Dirk looked impressed. "You know lots of folks around here, Will."

"Not so many. Just happened to come across a few of them now and then. Charles, how did this all start?"

"What I know is that General Beauregard sent Major Anderson a message at three thirty this morning, telling him this was his last chance. They all needed to abandon the fort or they would be fired on in one hour. Message from Anderson came back saying they weren't leaving. I think they were hoping the supply ships sitting just outside of the harbor would save them. They didn't leave, so we started firing at them. I say it's about time. They've had enough time and enough warnings. It's way past time for them to be out of here!"

"Guess they'll be leavin' now." Dirk smiled.

"They'll be running like scared rabbits soon enough," agreed Charles. "They don't belong here, and they know it. We'll send them back to mind their own business and tell Lincoln he can forget about Sumter! Good riddance, I say!"

"I hope you're right, Charles. I hope they do go back quick so we can all get back to bein' normal. From what I can see, looks like they're shootin' back, though."

"They won't be able to shoot for long, Will. They've only got about eighty-five men, and we got cannons firing at them from Fort Moultrie, Fort Johnson, Morris Island, and the floating battery. They can't last. This whole thing could be over with by the end of the day."

Charles turned back to watch the fireworks over the harbor. The sky was getting lighter, and it was easier to see the fort. For all the noise they were makin', it didn't look like they were doin' anything to the walls, like knocking them down. Then I remembered that Major Anderson told me that the walls were about five feet thick and made of bricks. I guessed that would take a lot of cannonballs.

"Hey, Will. You hungry?" I nodded, and we headed back toward the house.

• • •

Aunt Fran was ready for us. She had fresh muffins and a pot of grits on the stove. She and Miss Annie were drinkin' coffee at the table when we came in. "There certainly is a lot of cheering going on. Does it look like the fort is being destroyed, Will?" Miss Annie asked while she dabbed her eyes.

"No, ma'am. Actually looks like the fort is holdin' up real good."

"That is some small relief, anyway," she sighed. "I don't know how long they can hold out, but I'm most worried about somebody being killed. Especially Jefferson."

Aunt Fran put her arm around her and said, "Of course you are, dear. I'm sure they will be all right. Major Anderson seems like a level-headed commander. He won't let them get hurt if he doesn't have to."

Miss Annie looked at Aunt Fran and said, "I hope you're right. I have met the major, and he seems like he knows what he's doing."

"He has had a lot of experience, and I know he is compassionate. He will not let anything happen to his men if he can help it. I know this because someone I knew very well was with him in battle. The major takes care of his own." Aunt Fran looked at me and smiled, and I guessed that to mean that was all she was going to tell. It seemed to comfort Miss Annie.

Rhett spoke up with a mouthful of grits. "Aunt Fran, shouldn't we go home now and tell Ma and Mr. John that we all need to be careful?"

"I've thought about that, Rhett. What do you say we give them until tomorrow so they can get your house ready? I know they are out of danger because they are so far away. I also know that we are in no danger because Fort Sumter is three miles away, and none of those soldiers could come here."

"You know Pa is goin' to be real mad at you for not tellin' him and lettin' us stay."

"I am aware of that, Will. This isn't the way I would have liked our few days together to be. I was really thinking about picnics and playing games in the park, but this is how things have turned. When two people get married, they need to have a little time to get to know each other before they have a family with five children. Do you agree?"

"I guess so. Guess after we all move in together, it could get really busy for them."

"So, we'll wait until tomorrow like we planned, and I will take care of my brother's anger then. Now, I am going to ask you boys to find Joseph and see if there is anything you can do to help him out for a while this morning. I expect when the Hawkins get home they will want to have some sort of a party to celebrate because, I'm sure the Yankees will be gone by then."

I heard Miss Annie whisper, "I hope so."

• • •

We helped Joseph with a lot of little jobs during the rest of the day but kept listening to the cannons. Every so often, we would run out to the battery to ask folks how it was goin'.

"Those Yankees are putting up some fight!" said one man. "They aren't getting off too many shots, but they're not making it easy for us to drive them out. Let them fire off all of their ammunition, I say. When that's gone, they won't have a choice! Only thing is that when they do fire, they could hurt or kill somebody. I heard that a cannon just missed a hotel on Sullivan's Island near Fort Moultrie."

Later in the day, cannon fire from the fort was not nearly as often. They were gettin' pounded pretty bad from all sides that I could see. After one long pause from the fort, a cannon finally exploded, and even the Citadel cadets cheered. "They're still fighting! They sure are holding their own!" someone shouted.

The later it got, the more people left the battery. Lots of them had been there all night, and plenty of them were pretty drunk, too. The firin' slowed down. There was one shot from somewhere about every fifteen minutes, but the firin' from the fort stopped. I guessed they were all pretty tired and trying to get some rest to start again in the morning.

I was hopin' that it would all be over by morning. I knew I was ready to get some sleep.

CHAPTER 22

• • •

I WAS OUT OF BED just as the sky was startin' to lighten. I sure didn't sleep good, and I don't think anybody else did, either. I thought I heard Rhett cryin' some, and it looked like somebody was at the window when I woke up once. I guessed it was Dirk, but didn't care too much. I was still real tired.

When I did get downstairs, Aunt Fran was makin' some breakfast. "Oh, thank you, Fran, but I can't eat anything." It was Miss Annie. I know she didn't sleep at all.

"How about some tea, Annie?" Then Aunt Fran turned and saw me in the doorway. "Good morning, Will. I don't suppose you slept very well, either. Poor little Sarah was awake so much, I spent most of the night rocking her. Maybe I should have let you all go home yesterday. I had no idea that there would be cannons going off all night long. She fell asleep a short time ago. I hope it lasts. Are you ready for breakfast?" I nodded, but I couldn't believe how much Aunt Fran was doing. She was takin' care of us and not gettin' any sleep, either. It made me wish she had been able to have a family of her own.

I was just finishin' the biscuits and gravy when I heard, "Frances McShane! Where are you?" The kitchen door swung open, and Pa came stompin' in. I don't believe I've ever seen him like that. "What did you think you were doin' with my children?" he demanded.

"Good morning John. Morning, Mary. You are here earlier than I expected you." I couldn't believe she could stay so calm. I always got a little scared when Pa got mad.

"There ain't nothin' good about it! You get the young'uns down here right now. We're leavin'!"

Miss Mary moved in front of Pa. "Good morning, Fran. I'm sorry. I tried to convince him to wait, but he came as soon as he heard. One of the Wilson children came over early this morning to tell us what has been happening."

"That's all right, Mary. Will told me he would be upset."

"Don't you two be talkin' about me like I'm not here. Damn right, I'm upset!"

"John, there's no need to curse," Miss Mary said real sweet.

"There certainly isn't, John McShane! One thing you should understand by now"—I had never heard anybody talk to Pa like Aunt Fran was talkin'—"I love your children as if they were my own. I would never, never do anything that would put them in harm's way. Another thing. There has been talk going around for months about the fort and fighting. Did you think General Beauregard came to tell me personally that he was finally going to attack? If I knew this was going to happen, I wouldn't have suggested the children come here. Even so, have you seen all of the soldiers defending the city? Do you honestly believe they would let eighty-five half-starved men march into Charleston and take it over?"

By the time Aunt Fran was finished, Pa had calmed down some. "Well, I 'spect not. But that doesn't change anything. They should have come home yesterday."

"You're probably right, John. But let me ask you, did you and Mary enjoy your time together? Were you able to get the house finished for the children?"

"Yes, we did," Miss Mary told Aunt Fran. "We were able to get a lot done. I am looking forward to a visit from you so you can see it."

"That would be lovely, Mary."

"I don't understand women. There's a battle outside, and you two are talkin' about pretty houses." Pa shook his head.

Aunt Fran asked him, "What would you have us talk about, John? Cannons and guns? I think we'd like to focus on our lives and let the general take care of the battle. Now, how about some breakfast?"

We just got done with breakfast and were drinkin' our coffee when Dirk and Rhett came in. Rhett ran to Miss Mary and hugged her. "Ma, can I stay with you now? Can I come home with you?"

"Of course, Rhett. That's why John and I are here. To take you home."

I could see the relief on Rhett's face, but Dirk said, "Now? Why do we have to leave now? Those d—" He paused. "Those Yanks are just about beat, and I want to see it. Can't we stay?"

"Well, I expect you'll be staying for dinner, at least." Aunt Fran wasn't goin' to let us go too soon, I guessed.

Pa answered her, "Yes, Fran, we'll stay for dinner."

Dirk grabbed a biscuit and said, "Come on, Will. Let's go see what's happenin'!"

I looked at Pa. He nodded. "Guess this could be important," he said. "Go ahead, boys. I'll be out in a few minutes. I'd like to see what is happenin' out there for myself. I'd love to be able to wave good-bye to the Yankees so we can get back to farmin'." Miss Annie started cryin' again. "Sorry, Miss Annie. Didn't mean no disrespect."

"I know, Mr. McShane. I just feel so helpless, and it seems like I'm always crying lately." She sipped her tea through her tears.

Pa wasn't far behind us while we were headin' to the battery. "Sure is a dark cloud out there over the fort!" he screamed. He had to so we could hear him over the cheerin'. "Has it been like that the whole time?"

"No, sir!" I shouted back. "First time we seen anything like this!"

We heard folks shoutin' from the battery wall. "They're on fire! They'll surrender now! Let 'em burn!" We watched a while longer, and the crowd started settlin' down. Pa asked us what it had like here for the past two days. We were explainin' that sometimes it had gotten real loud and then seemed to quiet down for a while but that just as soon as we thought it was over, there would be a shot from Fort Sumter and it would start all over again.

Things at the fort seemed to get quiet while we were talkin', and just like before, when we figured they were ready to give up, a shell flew out toward Fort Moultrie. It was strange to me, but lots of folks were cheerin'. Somebody yelled, "They sure have gumption. They're still tryin' to fight!"

Dirk decided he needed to go back to have a proper breakfast, so Pa and I went with him. Pa said he would like another cup of coffee. I wouldn't mind havin' another biscuit myself.

Jacob and Sarah were both in the kitchen. Sarah was sittin' on Miss Mary's lap, finishin' her breakfast, and Jacob met us at the door. "What's happenin', Dirk? We heard more cheerin'."

Dirk looked around the kitchen. I think he was lookin' for Miss Annie. "Looks like they set the place on fire. They'll have to give up now, but they keep firin' back. Strange, too, because some folks on the battery sound like they're cheerin' *for* the Yankees."

"Do you think they might be showin' some respect? After all, only a few men have held off hundreds or maybe even thousands of soldiers after two days of shellin', and they're still tryin' to fight back. That shows some courage." Pa finished speaking just as Miss Annie walked back into the kitchen.

"Thank you, Mr. McShane. That's what I think, too," she said.

"I s'pose so," said Dirk. "But it sure puzzles me how come they just don't give up so they can go home safe."

Aunt Fran had been sittin' quiet for a time but couldn't seem to keep still no longer. "Dirk, you are still young. As you get older, you will learn that sometimes a man, or woman, may have some very strong feelings that they believe are worth defending even if it means giving up their life. That seems to be true especially about men who join the army. They feel like it is their responsibility to protect what their heart tells them is important. It could be an idea, like freedom, or it could be their home and family. These people seem to think it is necessary to work to accomplish that goal even if it means giving up their lives. Do you understand?"

"I guess so. I 'specially understand about protectin' your home and family."

Pa nodded and smiled at him. "Dirk, you're becomin' quite a man. Fran, I think I know who you're talkin' about."

"Don't start, John." She wiped her eyes, jumped up from the table, and said, "Mary, how would you like to help me start dinner? Annie, I could use your help, too, if you'd like. Rhett, would you and Sarah go out into the garden and pick a big mess of spinach? We can let the men go watch the fighting." She smiled. "We women have more important things to do." That was Aunt Fran's way of gettin' what she wanted. I know she likes to be busy, and she didn't want Pa talkin' about things that happened to her and Cyrus in the past. So we went back across the street.

It wasn't long before church bells started ringin' and people were cheerin' even louder. "Their flag is down! The Yankee flag is down! They've surrendered!"

We were near the battery wall where there was a man lookin' out with a spyglass like ship captains used. "The flag is down! There is a boat out there with a white flag flying, and it's heading toward the fort!" Guess he felt like he should tell all of us what they were doin' out there.

We waited for a while to see if the Yankees really did surrender, when he shouted again. "The flag is back up! What do they think they're doin?" Another shot was fired from the fort. "They're all crazy! They lost their minds! Wait…another boat is headed out from here with a white flag. What's going on?" It was quiet for a long time. The other boat had tied up at the fort. The man said soldiers got out and were talkin' with the Yankee soldiers.

Not too long after, the bells started again. "There goes the flag! They must have done it now! It's over! We whipped 'em! We beat the damn Yankees!" People were screamin' and huggin' all over the battery. Dirk and Pa and I got separated, and I got knocked down by a drunk man tryin' to hug me. I couldn't find the others, but I figured it was time to go back to the house. Celebratin' could be as dangerous as war!

Pa came in right after I did. "I'm glad this is over, but those folks sure are makin' fools of themselves!"

"Where's Dirk?" Miss Mary asked Pa.

"Don't know. We all got pushed apart when the flag came down the second time. I'm sure he'll be fine. He's got a good head."

Dinner was about ready when Dirk came in. His shirt was tore, and it looked like he got pushed down a few times, because he was so dirty. He had a real big smile on his face. "A girl kissed me, Ma, and I didn't even know her!"

Miss Mary looked at him funny, but I heard Pa say real quiet, "Mary, I said he was becomin' a man." She just nodded.

● ● ●

We were all sittin' at the table, eatin' dinner. Miss Annie was just sort of movin' food around on her plate, and we were pretty quiet because nobody wanted to make her cry again. Rhett and Sarah were doin' all the talkin' about all of the people they saw from the courtyard, when there was a knock on the door. We all jumped a little 'cause we weren't 'spectin' nobody.

Aunt Fran got up and said, "I wonder who that could be." When she opened the door, there was a soldier standin' there. Miss Annie gasped.

"Ma'am." The soldier sort of saluted. "I've been sent by General Beauregard with a message for Miss Annie Davis. Is she here?"

Miss Annie jumped up, almost trippin' on her way to the door. "That's me!"

"Miss Davis, the general sends his regards."

"That is kind, but I don't care about the general's regards right now. How is my brother?"

"Yes, ma'am. The lieutenant is fine. The general would like me to tell you that you will be leaving along with all of the soldiers tomorrow. You will all go back on the supply ship that came from New York. I have been assigned to come back first thing in the morning to pick you up. General Beauregard thought it would be best if the lieutenant stayed at the fort for his own safety."

Miss Annie was so relieved, I thought she would sink to the floor. "Oh, my. He wasn't hurt? Thank you so much. Wait. You said all of the soldiers are going back. Do you mean *all* of them?"

"Yes, ma'am. The surrender agreement included everyone being returned to New York. There were some injuries, but no one was killed. They all fought very bravely, if I do say so. You should be proud. Now I must get back to my duties. I will be here tomorrow."

Miss Annie did sink down into her chair. She started to cry again, and Sarah got down from her own chair, walked over to Annie, and held her hand. "Don't cry any more, Annie. Everything will be all right."

"Oh, Sarah." She hugged her. "You are so right. Everything is fine now. I guess I'm crying because I am so relieved. I must go finish packing!"

As she was leaving the room, Pa said, "Well, Miss Annie, I guess this is good-bye."

She stopped and turned around. "Oh, I won't be leaving until tomorrow."

"We'll be headin' home soon as we help Fran clean up here."

"Oh," she said quiet-like. "I didn't think of that."

"Pa, can we stay until they all leave tomorrow? We been here the whole time. We don't want to miss anything. And besides, if Miss Annie wants us to stay 'til tomorrow, we should, because she has helped so much with Sarah. You always said when somebody helps you, you should try to do them a kindness, and it seems that it would be a kindness to Miss Annie."

Aunt Fran even said, "Please, John. I'd feel so much safer with you here tonight. The crowd is so rowdy, and the Hawkins won't be back until tomorrow."

"John, the boys are growing up in a different time now. It could be important for them to experience the change."

"Now, don't you start, too, Mary. We got cows to milk and chickens to feed. The boys have seen enough."

"Please, Mr. John?" Jacob and Dirk said at the same time. "We'll take care of the animals tomorrow," added Jacob.

"What about Rhett and Sarah? They deserve some quiet."

"I don't care, Mr. Pa," said Rhett. We all looked at him. "What's wrong? Why is everybody starin' at me?"

"No reason, Rhett." Pa smiled.

"I want to see Annie!" Sarah was not goin' to be left out.

"Looks like I can't win this battle. I think I know how the Yankees feel." We all laughed. It felt good, because I don't think any of us had laughed in a long time.

"Now, boys, help me get cleaned up here," Miss Mary said. "Fran, would you like to help Annie? I'm sure you must have become very close."

"Thank you, Mary. When we finish, we can all have pie in the courtyard as a kind of farewell party for Annie."

It was dark when Miss Annie and Aunt Fran came down. We were all outside. The air was comfortable like usual this time of the year, and the azaleas all looked so pretty and smelled so good. I didn't seem to notice them before, but it seemed like they softened the bad time of the past two days. Aunt Fran's pie was as good as ever, but we were all gettin' real tired. We hadn't slept much the past few nights, and I didn't think tonight would be any different. With the crowds cheerin' and bells ringin', I figured it would be too loud to sleep, but Pa told us it was time to go up to bed.

Rhett wanted to stay with Miss Mary until she told him that she would come upstairs in five minutes to say good night and give him a kiss and that she wasn't goin' to be far at all. She did just that. We had all laid down when she came in. She went to Rhett's bed first, fixed his blanket, and gave him a kiss. She did the same to Jacob. She sat on a chair next to Dirk and talked to him for a while, real quiet. I don't know what she said, but it was soothin'.

Last, she stopped by me. "Will, I want you to know that I am very happy and feel very lucky to have you as one of my sons." She leaned over and kissed my forehead. I ain't felt like that in a long time. I closed my eyes.

CHAPTER 23

• • •

I GUESS THE NOISE FROM outside didn't bother me at all, because the next thing that happened was, Pa was waking me up and the sky was starting to get light. "Come on, Will," he said real quiet. "Miss Annie is about ready to leave, and she wants to say good-bye to you."

I got up as quiet as I could and made my way downstairs to the kitchen, where the lights were lit and coffee was smellin' like it was morning. "Thank you for getting up early, Will. I did want to say good-bye one more time. I have really enjoyed meeting you and your family." She had an extra big smile as she looked down at the still very sleepy Sarah. "I'm not sure if you know how often you two helped me get through this difficult time."

"I didn't do nothin', Miss Annie."

"Just being here and listening to me was a big help. I have waited for this for a long time, and now that it is here, I am a little sorry that I have to leave. You have all been so kind to me. Especially you, Fran. I owe you so much, I can't even think about how I could ever pay you back."

Aunt Fran smiled, but her chin quivered, and she wiped her eyes after she gave Miss Annie a hug.

The soldier that was standing in the doorway, waiting, cleared his throat and said, "Ma'am, we need to be going."

"Yes, I know. One more minute. Mr. and Mrs. McShane, I wish you and your new family all of the luck in the world. Will, I expect you to write to me soon!"

"I surely will. I am goin' to teach Sarah how to write so's she can send you a letter, too."

"That would be wonderful." She looked at Sarah, who was starting to cry. "Now, Sarah. No tears. I want to remember you smiling and all of the times you made me smile. Will you take care of your parents and all of your brothers for me and see that Will writes that letter?"

Sarah did smile, and she nodded. "I will, just as soon as we get home!"

"Good. Thank you all again, and good-bye. Oh...I almost forgot." She reached into her pocket and took out an envelope. "Fran, will you give this letter to Mr. and Mrs. Hawkins? They have been so gracious to share their home with me."

Then she was out the door, with the soldier following her to a buggy where her trunks were already loaded. We all waved until we lost sight of them in the crowd.

There were still people all over the park and the battery. Bonfires were dying down, and the people weren't real loud, but they weren't leaving, either. "How is she gettin' back, Pa?" I asked.

"Before I woke you, the soldier told me that they would take Miss Annie to a boat that would take her out to the ship that the Yankees are goin' back to New York on. He thought they would be gone by around noon."

"Why don't they leave right now?"

"General Beauregard is goin' to let Major Anderson and his garrison fire a hundred-cannon salute before they take down the US flag and turn over the fort to the Confederacy. I guess that's what they do in the army. The flag is an important symbol, and the general is goin' to allow the Yankees to honor it."

"A hundred cannons! They must all like the noise! Aunt Fran, is breakfast ready?" She smiled, and we went back into the house. I was looking forward to talkin' about our new family and not about the fort or war anymore, but I asked Pa if we could stay until they left?"

He nodded. "We stayed this long. I suppose we can wait a few more hours. Those cows are goin' to be awful mad, and you're feedin' the chickens. They'll be so hungry, they may attack your feet." We both laughed.

• • •

We had just finished eating when the others came down. Jacob said, "Hey, it isn't all gone, is it? I could smell breakfast all the way upstairs. Smells real good."

Aunt Fran got up from the table and got the fried pork and eggs. "Fresh biscuits are over there, boys. Get plates, and I'll dish this up for you."

Pa explained what had happened so far that morning and that we would be probably leaving around noon.

"It sure will be quiet around here," said Aunt Fran. "I'm glad the Hawkins will be back later today. I expect things will be busy after that. They'll probably want to have some sort of a celebration. They may even invite General Beauregard."

Dirk stopped his fork halfway to his mouth. "Really? They know the general?"

"Yes. It's not as if they are best friends, but they are strong supporters of the Confederacy. I wouldn't be surprised if Mr. Hawkins keeps in touch with him to offer any assistance that might be needed. The Hawkins know a great many people here in Charleston."

"Wow!" Then Dirk's fork finished its way to his mouth.

We sat around the table, talking about what we thought would happen next. Pa talked about clearin' more land for cotton. Miss Mary talked about her plans for more furniture and maybe some flowers by the front door. I was planning on doin' lots of readin' and teachin' Sarah some. I was hopin' that Jacob or Rhett could go to school with me again when Mrs. Wilson started it after harvest. I didn't figure Dirk would go, but I would try to talk him into it.

We all decided that Aunt Fran needed to come to visit us now. She said she would whenever she had the time to spend the day with us. That was usually when Mr. Hawkins was away on business trips. She wasn't sure if he would be traveling to New York anymore. Maybe he would just be doing business in the Confederacy.

After a time, Pa told us to go upstairs and put away what we had been using as beds. It was getting to be late in the morning, and he was planning on leavin' as soon as the hundred-cannon salute was over. "Nobody is goin' to talk me into stayin' one minute longer!" He looked stern, and we all knew that we had better be ready to go when he was.

By the time we came back down, the grown-ups were sittin' on the porch, watchin' the crowds across the street. They were some quieter, but they all wanted to stay to watch the Yankee flag come down off the fort.

Wasn't long before we heard a boom. We started countin'. Every few minutes, another cannon fired. I still couldn't believe that they were wastin' all those shells. Pa thought maybe it was a way Major Anderson could get rid of them so the Palmetto Guard or the South Carolina regiment couldn't get them. Whatever the reason, they just kept boomin'.

We were arguin' about whether we had heard forty-five or forty-six when there was a different kind of noise. It didn't sound like the other shots. It sounded more like an explosion. Then it was quiet. Nobody could figure out what happened.

Dirk and I ran across the street and pushed our way to the end of the battery to see if we could find out anything, but everybody was askin' and nobody was answerin'. Finally, it started again, but there were only three shells fired, and someone yelled, "They're taking down the flag! The Confederacy has won!" We could see the huge flag being lowered, and then it was gone. The cheerin' hurt my ears, but Dirk and I were cheerin' as loud as everybody else.

"Hooray for General Beauregard!" "Go home, damn Yankees!" "Nobody can beat the Confederate States of America!" The church bells started again. We were finally rid of the enemy!

It took us a while, but we made our way back to the house. Pa had Gray hitched up to the wagon, and the others were ready to leave. "What do you think happened that they only fired fifty times and not a hundred?" I asked Pa.

"I have no idea, Will. I do know that we are not goin' to stay around to find out. We are goin' home, and we are goin' now!"

"Yes, sir," Dirk and I said at the same time. We jumped into the wagon after givin' Aunt Fran a hug. We were on our way home.

It took a long time to get out of the city because of all the crowds and celebratin'. I wasn't sorry to be goin'. I'd seen about as much as I wanted to and now would like to spend some time fishin'.

"I expect everything is goin' to be good now, like Mr. Hawkins says, don't you think, Pa? I'm glad it's all over."

He was so quiet, I could hardly hear him when he said, "I hope you're right, Will, but I'm not so sure." And he just kept drivin' the wagon home.

Made in the USA
Columbia, SC
29 April 2017